IT HAPPENED ON JULY 18TH, 1995. I remember because it was my birthday. On July 18th, my dad crashed my mom's Grand Cherokee into a tree at the end of our driveway. Our property was so big the previous owners had built two tennis courts in the front yard. You drove up to the house on a gravel road and then along a tulip-lined circular driveway that curved past the veranda. The house was big, Victorian-style, and Granny Smith green with gray metal gables and an in-ground pool in the backyard. My dad had the tennis courts ripped out after he'd bought the place. They were for show-offs, he'd said. Besides, my mom had wanted flowerbeds put in.

It was about six in the evening when my dad smashed into my mom's favorite tree, a hundred-year-old oak. I'm not sure what kind of oak exactly because my mom knew nothing about trees. As for my dad, you couldn't even mention trees to him he despised them so much. He had to rake up a zillion dead leaves scattered across our property in the fall. It took three days even if I gave him a hand. Actually, I wasn't too helpful. My dad would complain that I was slacking off. He'd fill ten garbage bags for

7

every bag I filled. Eventually he'd get fed up and tell me to beat it and go play Nintendo. That summer, I spent almost every day trying to save Princess Peach from Bowser's Castle.

My dad had bought the jeep for my mom the year before. She chose fire-engine red. It'd be easier to find in the parking lot at the mall was what she told my dad at the car dealership. She wanted the red that was in the catalog, not the red of the demo that sat on iron beams in front of the store. The salesman told my mom her red had to be specially ordered. A jeep would need to be sent up from Montreal just for her, and it would cost my dad five thousand extra. She stared at the salesman and asked when her red jeep would arrive. She liked being special, and above all she liked having my dad cough up his money.

She was ecstatic when they left the dealership. My dad, though, was fuming. He asked what was wrong with the color of the store model since it was the same freaking red. My mom rolled her eyes and explained how the red in the catalog was brighter than the other red. There was an obvious difference. And she'd be the only one in Chicoutimi with a jeep that color. My dad shut up. He knew how to pick his battles. Anyways, he likely called the salesman behind my mom's back to cancel her special order. My mom would get the standard red, and she wouldn't even notice because she was dumber than a Chihuahua.

My mom fell out of love with her jeep pretty fast. My dad bought himself a second car that same year, a yellow Corvette, which my mom liked way better than the jeep. It was a sports car. My mom couldn't stand sports, but she went crazy over sports cars. She'd take me for drives on the highway in the Corvette. Once we'd hit the first curve, she'd put on her *Dirty Dancing* CD.

8

At "She's Like the Wind," she'd crank up the sound and push the pedal to 160. Meanwhile, I'd grip the door with all my might and wait for her goddamn song to end.

My mom wasn't in the jeep when it slammed into the tree. Only my dad was—my dad and his can of Labatt Blue. The Labatt was an accident, though. My dad would never drink and drive, but he just happened to have a beer in his hands when he decided to total the jeep.

I remember that on the afternoon of my birthday, the kitchen table was piled high with like forty-two different things for my party. Styrofoam cups, paper plates and matching napkins, balloons, plastic tablecloths, party hats, bags of chips. My mom had gone nuts at the dollar store—no surprise there. I checked in the fridge to make sure she'd bought some Sunny Delight. It was basically the only thing I cared about for my party. Me and Vanessa Dubois needed our SunnyD. I'd finally get permission to go to the mall on Thursday nights. My parents thought thirteen-year-old girls that hung out at Royal Plaza were little sluts, but apparently once you turned fourteen, it was no biggie. At the mall, we'd empty out half the SunnyD and fill the bottle with vodka. Vanessa had seen in some murder mystery on TV that vodka was the only booze that couldn't be smelled on your breath.

On the morning of my birthday, my parents got into a huge blowout. My dad had come in at four in the morning because he'd taken some clients of his to a strip club. My mom was royally pissed. She hated strippers. They were cheats who'd rob men blind. My dad claimed he'd ended up there because of his clients. It was always the same story. The guys from Montreal wanted to see strippers when they came up to the Saguenay without their wives.

9

How could he say no? They were big clients. My mom had better stop her bitching right then and there, he said, because thanks to those big shots we got to travel south three times a year.

My mom jumped my dad. While they were wrestling around, she clawed at his arms and called him an asshole. She had long fingernails like in fashion magazines. Her beautician had told her all the girls in Europe had a French manicure, and my mom had hers done every week. Nails like that required tons of upkeep.

The salon was in a tiny mall on Racine Street right under Gagnon Brothers. My mom would leave her car in the parking garage. She'd hurry in because she was terrified of the bums who slept on the staircase near the entrance. There was always at least one, and it'd smell like piss. That was why she wouldn't cut through the inside and instead would go down in the elevator for the handicapped way at the other end. At the same time, she could check if the waterbeds were on sale at Gagnon Brothers. She'd told me she was shopping for one for Christmas.

By the time my dad had my mom under control, he had a tear in his shirt, a swollen eye, and scratches up and down his arms like he'd been attacked by a wolverine. He was used to my mom's hysterics. He said she'd go apeshit like that because she had native blood in her. These fights always played out the same: my mom would jump my dad, he'd let her freak out and pummel him a bit, and then he'd push her up against a wall to make her stop. Then she'd go even crazier. She might spit in his eye and call him names. After a couple minutes, she'd finally cool down. Then my dad would let her go. He'd slowly ease his grip because sometimes she'd pretend to calm down just so she could smack him again. Afterward, she'd lock herself in her room and bawl for an hour or two. When I couldn't hear her whimpering anymore, I'd bring her a glass of water. My dad would send me. He'd first warn me to be careful in case she mistook me for him, but I wasn't scared of my mom and her fake native blood. That story about her Innu grandma was bullshit. The lady at the welfare counter had told her so when she'd tried applying for an Indian status card to pay less tax.

That morning, my dad went off to run errands while my mom was shut up in her room. Usually after a blowout, he'd stick around just in case. After a family party, my mom had kicked in a closet door and broken a mirror. She'd come out of her bedroom with a big shard of glass in her hand and chased my dad around the house threatening to shove it up his ass. My dad had slept with his secretary, and my mom had caught him. Ever since then, my dad would stick close to home.

But the morning of my birthday, my dad was furious with my mom. It was true she'd gone too far. She never managed to seriously hurt my dad though, except maybe the time when he'd set her terrycloth underwear on fire while she was doing the dishes. My dad snuck up behind her with his lighter while she was scrubbing a pan. He lit a thread that was hanging down her thigh and then the little nubs of terrycloth all got singed at once. My mom turned around and walloped him with her cast-iron pan, splitting his forehead open. The doctor who later sewed him up gave him a brochure on domestic violence, but my dad threw it in the trash on his way out of the ER.

My mom came out of her room around ten o'clock. She looked a mess because her mascara had run and her lipstick had smeared across her cheeks. As she wiped off and then reapplied

11

her makeup, she wondered how my dad could be such a jerk on my birthday. I liked watching her put on makeup. While she did her face, she'd tell me stories about her modeling days. She'd been prettier back then. At age eighteen, she'd modeled in Los Angeles, which she called "L.A." In L.A., she'd seen Elvis Presley buying a motorcycle at the end of her street. The whole neighborhood went to crowd around Elvis, but not my mom. She knew she was pretty, but not pretty enough for the King.

When she finished her makeup, my mom started setting up for my party. She laid the plastic tablecloth over the patio table and put out the paper plates and matching cups. I'd asked her to make Chinese food. I helped her marinate chicken cubes and hot dogs in VH sauce to make skewers. We'd grill them at around five o'clock, and Vanessa Dubois would even be invited over. I didn't know if she liked Chinese food, though, and I remember I was worried about that. I kept thinking if Vanessa didn't like Chinese skewers and Uncle Ben's rice, my party would be a drag.

Around three, my dad came back from shopping, but with no shopping bags. He'd obviously just gone to the bar and spent the day there. When my mom saw him, she pretended everything was normal. She didn't give a fuck that my dad had been out drinking, especially since the two of them had gotten into a brawl that morning. She was more forgiving at times like that. My dad trudged down to the basement. He came back up with a six-pack of Labatt Blue, wished me happy birthday, and handed me a can of beer. Awesome. I wondered if I'd get lots of new privileges. Just then, Vanessa showed up, but my dad didn't offer her a beer because he was afraid her parents wouldn't approve. She didn't care. I gave her a few quick gulps of mine while we were in the swimming pool. The beer tasted pretty lousy, but I drank it to make my dad happy. My birthday would turn out okay after all, and Vanessa loved Chinese food. She told me and my mom just before we served the skewers. Plus, it was beautiful out, like every July 18th.

After dinner, it was time to open my presents. I couldn't wait to unwrap the gift with the polka-dot paper and the big stupid bow. My mom kept a box of bows in the basement and was always bringing bows home. At my godmother's birthday the year before, my mom had nabbed a big one and stuck it in her purse, and now it was on my present. Vanessa whispered that my gift was probably a Discman. It had to be since I'd been begging for one for like six months. My dad was slumped in his patio chair and looked sloshed. He kept shooting my mom weird glances, and I wondered if he was still pissed at her. Vanessa was right: my gift was a yellow Panasonic Shockwave Discman. I quickly unwrapped my other two presents, which were less impressive. One was an ugly pair of pajamas covered in teddy bears like what a six-year-old would wear. The other was a book: *Christiane F.* I actually couldn't wait to read it, but how strange that my mom gave me a book about a thirteen-year-old junkie hooker. I thanked my mom and dad. My dad stood up and said there was one more present coming, and my mom got this confused look on her face. My dad came to the table and took out his checkbook and then his Montblanc pen, which he used for signing his big business contracts and my report cards. He ripped out a check, wrote on it, folded it in half, and handed it to me. Vanessa didn't know what to do with herself. She stood up to clear the table, but my mom snapped at her to sit back down. I unfolded the check. My mom asked how much it was for. A thousand bucks. I was totally stunned. With that kind of cash, I could buy like anything I wanted at the mall. All kinds of makeup, every Nirvana CD, the dress in the window of Le Château, fishnet stockings, a pair of burgundy Docs, bikinis to wear down south, a bomber jacket. If I had any money left, I'd even buy a couple movies. Me and Vanessa had been dying to see *The Evil Dead*. Maybe my dad would let us watch it on his new big-screen TV.

It wasn't the first time my dad had given me money while he was drunk, and my mom wasn't happy one bit. Was he out of his fucking mind? You didn't give a thousand dollars to a kid. It was insane. My dad muttered that my mom was the insane one and that she was just jealous of me because I was prettier and she wanted the thousand bucks for herself. He stormed inside without closing the patio door.

Not long after, a loud crash came from the front yard. Me, Vanessa and my mom sprang up and ran to see what had happened. At the end of the driveway, my mom's jeep had bashed into the huge oak tree next to Mrs. Sorensen's property. My dad pulled himself out of the wreck, blood running from his nose. He staggered around. Then he pointed at the jeep, smiled at my mom, and gave her the finger. The jeep was totaled. Me and Vanessa went and holed up in my room and let them fight it out. I really didn't give two shits. I had my SunnyD and I knew I'd be going to the mall on Thursday.

My parents gave each other the silent treatment till the end of August. They tried not to cross paths at home. My dad was working crazy hours and taking on extra cases at his law firm. Meanwhile, my mom kept inviting her sisters and her ditzy friends over for girls' night, which would drag on really late. My dad hated those ladies and would sleep at the office whenever they came over. I think my mom invited them just to teach my dad a lesson.

My mom had been calling my dad an egomaniac and an alcoholic since I was like four years old. My dad, though, would never badmouth my mom to me. In fact, he didn't talk to me much at all. Sometimes I'd be fed up hearing my mom call my dad a drunk and a manipulator, so I'd go sit with my dad in the living room. We'd watch *The Hunt for Red October*, his favorite movie. He'd rent it like six times a year. One time, this clerk at the video store had suggested my dad buy it instead of renting it. When my dad asked why, the clerk explained that buying the video would cost less than renting it six times. My dad was insulted. He didn't buy the thing. We even went to another video store and opened an account there. No way would he go back to the first store with that fucking snarky little bastard. In fact, he'd gone to school with the clerk's father and planned to go see the man the next day to tell him his son had no manners. The guy owned the Ultramar gas station in our neighborhood.

My mom waited till my dad was off hunting moose in September to announce to me that we were moving out. I was surprised because her and my dad had started talking again and going out to dinner together. I'd even heard them having sex the week before.

My parents didn't make love too often. I'd overheard my dad complain about it a while back. It was around four in the morning, and they'd gone to a restaurant that night. I knew they'd had a few rounds of Brazilian coffees because my mom told my dad it was the brandy talking. My dad said he was so damn tired of beating off and that if my mom kept holding out, he'd sleep with another secretary. My mom laughed and called him needle dick. That shut him up.

My mom had already started looking for an apartment for us and said she could use my help. We didn't need men in our lives, she insisted. She'd get a job. She hadn't worked in like fourteen years, but a friend's husband, an accountant, needed a secretary and was willing to hire my mom. If she worked for the accountant, we could still travel to Florida three times a year like before. We'd move into a place that was smaller than our house, but just as luxurious. Everything would be the same, only my dad wouldn't be around to hassle us.

My mom told me to look through the classifieds for a place with two bedrooms. Also, it had to be brand new. The paper didn't advertise many apartments like that. No way would my mom move into some cruddy place with parquet floors and venetian blinds. We visited three apartments. The supers who showed us around called them condos, and a condo was exactly what me and my mom wanted.

One day when we got back from seeing a condo, my dad's pickup was parked in the driveway. It was four days before his hunting trip was supposed to end. He obviously hadn't killed anything because there was no moose head sitting on the hood of his pickup. When my mom saw my dad come out of the house, she went as white as a ghost. She told me to go straight inside and up to my room. I put a Lagwagon CD in my Discman and waited. I had time to listen to the album three times before my mom came to get me. Her mascara and lipstick were all smeared as usual. She told me some guy who had his hunting blind near my dad's had asked him why his wife was visiting condos. The guy knew because we'd looked at an apartment a week before in a building he owned and he'd seen my mom's name on the form for the credit check.

Well, my dad had a total meltdown. Still, he went back to the Valin Mountains that night. Going out the door, he yelled at my mom to take her daughter and her clothes and get the fuck out. He said if we were still there when he came back from the woods, he'd shoot her in the head. He was talking tough because he was in a rage, my mom said. That was how men were. They'd yell horrible things and then feel all sorry later, and that was the best time to go after what you wanted—big alimony payments, the house, the Corvette.

Except my mom was wrong. When he came back from hunting three days later, my dad was even more pissed than before. He'd booked a room at the motel, and then he drove over the next day to ask my mom why we were still in his house. I didn't catch everything they said to each other. They shut themselves in my dad's office, and two minutes later I heard my mom yell she hadn't passed the credit check for the condo. She wasn't about to move into a dinky studio apartment just to make him happy. My mom came back out and started unloading the dishwasher. I snuck into the office to see my dad, and he was on the phone with the guy who had a hunting blind near his. He said he'd sign for my mom and that the guy should let us move in. My dad hung up and brushed past without even looking at me. I followed him to the kitchen. He grabbed a dish out of my mom's hands and kicked the dishwasher closed, causing glasses to break in the top rack. He turned to me and my mom, and he had the same face as when he'd caught his partner embezzling the year before. He said we'd never swindle him out of his house, and especially not his Corvette. We could just take the bus like all the other fucking losers. As for alimony, the lawyers could hash it out, but my mom had better not get her hopes up because he didn't plan on giving her a dime.

We moved the week after. The condo was in a neighborhood called the Swallows, an area I knew because the bus to the mall would wind through its streets to pick up the old farts who lived in the apartment blocks there. We'd live in a new development that had no trees. We'd have a swimming pool, though, but we'd share it with the owners of the other condos and I was embarrassed to go swimming with strangers. My dad painted the apartment because my mom had no money left for a contractor. She'd blown her entire line of credit on new furniture from Gagnon Brothers and on a decorator. While my dad was painting the ceiling, he kept coughing and rubbing his eyes like the fumes were toxic. I felt bad for him. I knew he loved my mom and was sorry he'd thrown us out.

My parents had first met when my mom got back from L.A. In the condo, she'd tell me their story whenever she showed me her modeling portfolio. At first, she'd been tall and slim with long hair dyed blond. She looked like a cheaper version of Brigitte Bardot. By the time we reached the middle of the album, though, she was still a tall brassy blonde, but also really chubby. Ice cream was why. She ate a bowl every night with her roommate. Americans made the best ice cream in the world, she said.

After six months, my mom had gained twenty pounds, and then casting agents stopped calling. The last contract she had was for a company that made spark plugs for chainsaws. It was supposed to be a bikini shoot, but when the client finally saw her, he decided to put her in a light orange jumpsuit with the company logo sewn on. He insisted she'd still look gorgeous, but my mom knew better. She hightailed it back to Quebec that same week, and soon afterward she met my dad.

At the time, he'd just passed his bar exams and needed a secretary to book his appointments and take his suits to the cleaner's. He put an ad in the paper, and my mom was the first to apply. She'd gone to secretary school. My grandma, who was always thinking ahead, had made her enroll in case her modeling career was a flop. My mom had wanted to become a stewardess, but my grandma said no way because stewardesses were whores.

My mom wasn't the best secretary in the world, but she was pretty and she knew how my dad took his coffee. Plus, since getting home from California, she'd laid off the ice cream and bought a stationary bike. After two months, she had her old figure back—her slim waist and big boobs. Not long after he hired her, my dad divorced his first wife and then moved with my mom into a big house off Doctor Lake. I was born seven months later. We moved away when I was three months old because my mom was scared I'd drown in the lake.

My mom was chatting away about her past as I was getting ready for the mall. I tried cutting her off so I wouldn't miss the bus, but she kept rattling on. She whined that I was leaving her alone again and that I liked my friends better than her. If I wasn't careful, I'd wind up like Christiane F., she said. Oh, for chrissake, I wasn't some poor waif whose dad smacked her around. And good luck finding any heroin in Chicoutimi.

ME, VANESSA AND Sarah Duperré started hanging out at the mall on both Thursday and Friday nights. Royal Plaza was divided in two: the Ardene side and the Canadian Tire side. Me and my friends stayed on the Ardene side with the skaters. It was the best end of the mall because the food court was there, and so were the cute guys. We could spend two hours sitting at the little tables in front of Dunkin' Donuts eating nothing and drinking our SunnyD-vodka mix. Unless the security guards told us to get lost, we'd hang out there and watch Pascal Tremblay and his buddies go by with their Airwalks and their Quiksilver T-shirts. Pascal was the coolest of them all since he snowboarded and bleached his hair. He looked like Kurt Cobain or Jay Adams even though he had zits. Later, we'd walk around our end of the mall and yell insults at girls we didn't like the look of.

The Canadian Tire side was for the skids with their mullets and wispy mustaches who drove over from Falardeau and tried looking all superior. They'd always have on white Sugi sneakers and Slayer T-shirts. Instead of winter coats, they'd wear Arctic

Cat snowmobile jackets. I remember they were total white trash.

On Fridays, we could come home later because it wasn't a school night. After closing time, me, Vanessa and Sarah would bum around the field behind the mall. Sarah was always scared because she was a big wuss and her parents thought perverts hung out there. I wondered why Vanessa put up with Sarah. Maybe she was lonely ever since I'd moved away. Anyhow, we'd watch the skaters get into fights with the skids. There were lots of fights between the two sides back then, so many in fact that the police kept watch over the field and patrolled every half-hour to tell us to move along.

One Friday, things went way, way too far. At least six hundred kids gathered behind the mall for a fight. Our brawl even made the front page of the local paper the next day. It was the biggest fight between skaters and skids of all time, and it started because one of the skaters had stolen the girlfriend of this skid from Shipshaw. The skids drove into town with baseball bats and crowbars. The skaters knew they were coming because the skids' leader, a guy called Jessie or some other hick name, had told a friend of the girlfriend that he'd kill the skater dude. The girlfriend then blabbed to everybody at school. Our side headed to the bus station after school to rally as many people as possible. Afterward, Pascal and two or three other guys waited for Jessie outside the adult-ed school to say they'd rounded up a thousand kids to be at the mall that night. Jessie and his gang of homos wouldn't believe it. No way could I not go. Me and Vanessa couldn't wait to slap around a few of those skid bitches in their crop tops.

The mall closed at nine. By nine-fifteen, there were at least two hundred cars parked all around. People had left their car doors open and were blasting their music in a kind of stereo war. As everybody waited for the fight to start, guys were guzzling Bull Max and egging each other on. Me, Vanessa and Sarah started getting a bit scared. More and more cars kept coming, kids were arriving on foot from the woods out back, and gangs of guys we'd never laid eyes on before were riding around the field on their BMX bikes. Vanessa pointed out a group of Indian chicks with big hair who were getting out of this clunker of a car. We thought they were from the Blue Point reserve. Things were getting totally out of hand, and Sarah said she wanted to go home. We found out later that those Indians were just some bimbos from Chicoutimi North. Anyways, I told Sarah to take off because she'd been whining for like twenty minutes. She went to call her mother to come get her, and we didn't see her for the rest of the night, which was a relief really. I was staying put, though. I'd just spotted Melanie Belley. I hated that cow because she thought she was so hot with her white Neon and the exact style of Lois jeans I wanted. Plus, she was Pascal Tremblay's girlfriend. I didn't get what he saw in her. She had a gut and wore her makeup like some heavy-metal chick with a dark blue line drawn under her eyes, but not on her eyelids. She was probably sleazy like the girls from St. Jean Eudes High School.

All of a sudden, a bunch of cop cars sped down Talbot Boulevard with their lights flashing. The mall's security guards must've called them. About twenty cars, a paddy wagon and three ambulances drove up, but it was too late to disperse the crowd and stop a brawl.

The skaters had crossed over to the skids' side and were calling them cocksuckers. Then all hell broke loose. Two hundred guys started throwing punches, and it was hard to tell who was on which side. A cop yelled into his megaphone, but you couldn't hear a damn thing. Everybody went fucking ballistic. Pascal Tremblay was smacking a guy from St. Honoré in the face with his skateboard while another skid was whipping Pascal with a wallet chain. Then two more skids started pummeling Pascal with their baseball bats. God knows how many times they whacked him, but later Pascal was carried off the field on a stretcher and I heard the other dude spent a week in a coma.

While the skaters and the skids were fighting, the girls on both sides kept screaming at each other. We called one another slut, the worst insult ever for a girl. At one point, I'd pushed Melanie Belley too far, and she started harassing me in that dopey voice of hers. After a half-hour of that, I finally jumped her. I never figured out exactly what happened after, even though Vanessa told me a hundred times. The thing was, Melanie had four brothers and her father had taught them all to box when they were barely out of diapers. One of the brothers got to be a famous boxer in the region. He was ten years older than Melanie and dragged her around with him everywhere. She sold T-shirts and mugs with his face plastered on them whenever he had boxing matches at the arena. He'd also taught her how to use a punching bag, so I really got clobbered. She kicked me in the crotch and gave me an uppercut like a guy. I fell back and didn't have time to scramble up before she sat her fat ass down on me. I could barely breathe. I tried yanking a handful of her hair, but she slugged me in the face. I expected to see my life flash before my eyes, but I didn't. Two policewomen pulled her off. I can't remember much else. Vanessa said that when she carted me home, my mouth was bleeding and a sleeve of my jacket was torn half off. As for Melanie, she just had a few scratches across her face. My mom had a fit when she opened the door and saw me. I ended up spending the night with a bag of frozen peas pressed against my cheek.

When we moved into the condo, I never dreamed Melanie Belley would be at the same bus stop as me every morning. She lived in the public housing near our new place, and whenever we drove by the building my mom would sigh and ask what the hell a housing project was doing in the Swallows. It was a fairly new practice for the city to build public housing outside the shittier neighborhoods.

Since the night of the fight, my school mornings always started out the same way: Melanie would plant herself at the bus stop and scowl at me till the bus came. As we got on, she'd shove me hard and then go sit at the back with two other girls, who'd also give me the evil eye. I remember I was scared shitless whenever I'd run into Melanie, especially since she'd told everybody at school she'd kick my teeth in if she ever caught me at the mall again.

Well, I went back to the mall the next Thursday, and the bitch was standing right outside Ardene. She yelled my name. At first, I thought she meant another Catherine, but she was looking right at me, so I had no choice but to face her, even though I wasn't in the mood for another split lip. Melanie was with the same two girls in pigtails as on the bus, two puck bunnies in jean jackets. She spoke so loud that shoppers all around turned to look. We were cool, she said. She wanted a truce. I didn't understand, so I asked her what the deal was. She came over to me and when she saw my face up close, she said with a laugh that she'd gone a bit overboard. Maybe she wasn't such an asshole after all. She invited me to go to McDonald's with her and her friends. I wanted to go, but I hesitated. Was it some trick to lure me there and then beat the crap out of me? Melanie said to chill. A girl at school had told her I was pretty nice, and a friend of Pascal's thought I was cute and asked her to lay off me. In that case, I'd go to McDonald's with them, I said.

When we got there, we ordered two fries and a Coke for four, but the lady behind the counter told us we couldn't loiter, that it said so on the sign outside. If we wanted to stay, we all needed to buy something. The pigtail chicks asked for Happy Meals with the toy for girls. Excellent choice, I thought. The lady practically threw our food at us. We went and sat at the back of the restaurant, and Melanie told us she was thinking about breaking up with Pascal because on the weekend she'd met a new guy named Simon who was way cuter. He had a dirt bike and played the drums. We all agreed that if a guy played the drums in a punk band, you went out with him. I decided if Melanie dumped Pascal, I'd go up and talk to him at the mall.

The girls got up and asked if I'd go with them to the restroom. I said yeah, so we went and locked ourselves in the handicapped stall because it was way roomier there. I'd heard at school that Melanie snorted mescaline and I felt like trying it. She took a baggie out of her purse, and I knew what it was because I'd once seen a girl snort mesc. Melanie emptied the baggie on top of the toilet tank and made lines with her student card. Then she rolled up a five-dollar bill, and I inhaled two lines. I'd read about snorting in *Christiane F.*, so I pretended I was an expert. Afterward, I didn't feel much, except my nostrils burned. Still, I faked being stoned.

The next morning at school, everybody was staring at me as I arrived at my locker. Melanie and her friends were sitting on a bench just opposite. I unlocked my lock and hung up my jacket. I had math first period and had to get a move on because the teacher hated us coming in late. His name was Mr. Martel, and he was a complete psycho. I gathered my books, locked my locker, and went up to the girls to walk with them. One of the pigtail chicks called me a fucking idiot. Melanie had tricked me into snorting baking soda mixed with crushed Tic Tacs.

At school, I was now a total reject. Vanessa and Sarah were the only ones still talking to me. When I'd see Melanie in the hall, she'd shove me into the lockers or yell to everybody to make way for the big fake. Though I tried to avoid her, I kept running into that chick. One afternoon at the end of gym class, Melanie emptied my whole gym bag on the floor while I was in the showers. When I came out to get dressed, my clothes were scattered all over the locker room. Melanie started jeering at me, asking if I'd been in a toilet stall snorting mesc again. Was it good shit? Who was my dealer? The cunt had my Discman in her hands. I told her to stop being a jerk and hand it over, but she went and locked herself in a stall and threw my Discman in the toilet. She flushed to make sure it was wrecked for good.

The next few days, I faked a stomach ache to skip school. I didn't want to see Melanie at the bus stop and was fed up with everybody picking on me. At first, my mom let me miss class, but on Friday she made me fess up about what was going on. Well, she flipped out, ordered me into the car, and then ran three stop signs on Bégin Street.

When we got to school, she marched off to the principal's office at such a fast clip I could hardly keep up. She brushed past the secretary without looking at her and just barged into the principal's office. I was mortified. She was acting like such a hick. The principal was on the phone with God knows who. He waved for us to sit down and told whoever was on the phone that he'd call back later. He smiled at me and asked my mom if she had an appointment. No, she did not. The principal glanced at his watch. It was okay. He'd make time for us. That calmed my mom down because she liked when people made an exception for her. He pushed a button on his intercom and told his secretary not to disturb him. My mom started explaining, but I didn't listen much because I was staring at the principal's shoes, which looked brand new. They were black and white saddle shoes. They were seriously cool, like the shoes worn by the gangsters in *Scarface*. They didn't look at all like a principal's shoes, but I had to stop daydreaming about Al Pacino because my mom wanted to know the name of the delinquent who'd been harassing me for two weeks. Melanie Belley. Saying her name stressed me out. I hated snitches. I knew that within ten minutes the entire school would find out. My mom asked the principal what a girl like Melanie Belley was doing in his school anyway. Besides bullying her daughter, the little witch was likely selling drugs. He'd look into the drugs, the principal said, and he'd also call Melanie's parents in for a talk. My mom seemed satisfied and told him I'd be back in class on Monday.

On Monday, Melanie came to school with her parents. She glared at me like she wanted to slit my throat, and then she slunk off to the principal's office. I went to math class but didn't have time to open my textbook before my name was called over the PA. I got up and gathered my things. Everybody turned to gape. The teacher told me to hurry up, that he didn't have all day. When I walked into the principal's office, I saw Melanie, her head hung low. Her parents sat side by side, her mother sniffling and her father furious. The principal asked Melanie if she had anything to say to me. She was sorry, she muttered, staring at the floor. The principal gave me permission to go back to class and said I wouldn't have any more trouble with Melanie.

After the last bell, she was waiting for me at my locker. I was dead meat, she said. I went home and called my mom an idiot. She'd gotten me into deeper shit by dragging me to see the principal. She was always fucking everything up, I said. My mom slapped me across the face, and I sprang at her. We started grappling, and I twisted her pinkie and clawed her neck. My mom let out a weird shriek and ran off to lock herself in her room. She called my dad. She was yelling and crying into the phone, saying I'd gone totally psycho and that she didn't want me under her roof another minute. He'd have to come get me. Well, I couldn't wait to pack my bags.

But my dad refused to come. My mom would have to deal with me. It was her fault if I was a crazy bitch like her. My dad must've hung up on her because I heard something—probably the phone—crash against the wall. My mom stormed out and ordered me to my room to think things over. I told her to fuck off, and she started crying again. She had the same face as when she tried manipulating my dad. She looked kind of pitiful, but I chewed her out anyway. She was a fucking cow, I yelled. Because of her, I was stuck living in a crappy condo and my dad wanted nothing to do with me. I started crying and ran off to my room. I slammed the door and then started bashing my fist against the wall till the drywall caved in. My knuckles were throbbing and all scraped. My mom barged in because she'd heard the pounding and was scared I'd kill myself like Kurt Cobain. She went and got her first-aid kit, which she'd obviously never opened before because she rooted through it like a lunatic for Band-Aids and Mercurochrome. I told her I needed an elastic bandage. She rolled white cotton gauze around my hand, but it was so tight I couldn't move my fingers except for my pinkie. She didn't say a word the whole time. She must've been really bummed because usually she couldn't keep her big mouth shut.

The next day, my dad came to repair the drywall. He told me he loved me. He'd never said anything like that before. We were in my room, and I was holding the bucket of plaster, and then my dad put his trowel down and started to cry. He wrapped his arms around me. I was his little girl, he said, and he loved me more than anything in the world. I remember that his hug weirded me out and I just wanted him to let me go.

On Saturday, Pascal invited me to a movie. *Dangerous Minds* had just come out. I didn't get why he was phoning—some trick of Melanie's, no doubt. I told him to leave me alone, I couldn't take any more of that crap, but he cut me off. He'd broken up with Melanie. She was too damn crazy. Anyways, he'd been wanting to talk to me for a while. It was kind of cute because he sounded shy over the phone. The line went quiet, and I wondered if he was still there. Finally, he spoke up: Would I go with him? I said okay. He'd pick me up in his father's car.

As soon as I hung up, I wondered what I'd wear. The burgundy dress I'd just bought at Le Château? The wool jumper from Limité? I had to look sexy, but not sleazy, so the jumper would be better. I didn't have tights to wear with it, though. I went to ask my mom to lend me a pair, and she wanted to know what for. I was going to the movies with a boy. My mom asked me his name and what his father did. Pascal Tremblay, I said. His father was a big shot at the Alcan plant.

Pascal came by at seven-thirty in a humongous Dodge Ram, which he'd just run through the car wash. I'd waited for him outside. It was snowing—a light, cold October snow that melted down my neck—and I was worried my hair would go flat. Pascal jumped out of his pickup with his snowboard jacket unzipped. He was still a little bruised from the fight behind the mall, and he also looked shorter than usual. He was all clean and tidy, but I had to laugh because he was wearing a Lacoste polo with skater pants. I gave him a kiss on the cheek. He smelled good, like Bounce. He opened the door for me, and I held his arm as I climbed into the pickup. Once we drove off, I had him crank up the heat. He asked what I wanted to listen to. The Offspring, I said.

At the movie theater, a good half-hour of *Dangerous Minds* went by before Pascal pretended to stretch and then draped his arm around my shoulders. My heart started thumping because I knew we'd make out. I was so glad I hadn't ordered Doritos. He kissed me just when Michelle Pfeiffer announced to her class of black kids that she'd invite the winner of her poetry contest out to this ritzy restaurant. Michelle Pfeiffer wasn't nearly as pretty as she'd been in *Scarface*, and the movie dragged on forever, but I didn't care because Pascal had his hand down my sweater and it felt good. Afterward, we went to HMV in the mall to buy the CD with the theme song from the movie. We were really into it even though rap wasn't usually our thing. We bumped into Baptiste Amadou, who was buying a Dr. Dre CD, and him and Pascal chatted a bit. Baptiste was as hot as the guy from *Dangerous Minds*. I wasn't the only girl who thought so. He was the only black dude in Chicoutimi, and after that movie came out, he got laid all the time.

On Monday morning, Melanie was waiting for me at my locker. Her mascara had run, and she looked like Alice Cooper. She'd murder me if I ever went out with Pascal again, she said. I gave her the finger and walked off to English class. While the teacher was explaining the difference between "who" and "whom," I wondered how the hell Melanie had found out about my date with her ex-boyfriend. The only person I'd told was Vanessa. Pascal likely spilled the beans to Melanie so she'd leave him the fuck alone. That was what I hoped anyway. All I knew was I wasn't scared of that bitch anymore. Between English and geography, I went out to see if Vanessa was smoking in the woods behind the school. I didn't find her. Instead, I ran into the Happy Meal girls, but this time they didn't hassle me. One of them even said she liked how I was wearing my hair that day.

In the cafeteria at noon, Melanie threw a Granny Smith apple at my lunch tray. It fell into my mushroom soup, which splashed all over my sweater. Melanie's friends said she was being a bit of a retard throwing apples around. She needed to get over Pascal, they said. What did she care if I was seeing him? After all, she was going out with Simon now. Melanie came over with some napkins and said she was sorry, and since she had a pouty dog face, I could tell she wasn't kidding around. It was okay, I could have Pascal, she said. I should stop wearing Kickers, though, because I looked like a dork in them. Kickers hadn't been cool since the sixth grade, she said. I had to buy Airwalks and wear them with patterned socks from Jacob. I thought Airwalks were freaking ugly on a girl, and Jacob socks were for losers. Did I go telling her that her big tits looked droopy in that top she was wearing? I wanted eight-hole Doc Martens and striped knee socks like the girls in the NOFX videos. I'd wear them with a short plaid kilt held together with a giant safety pin, and also a No Use for a Name T-shirt for girls. Another thing I wanted was a Face to Face sweatshirt, but it cost too much, and my mom wouldn't spring for it, especially after I'd burned through the thousand bucks from my dad in two weeks flat.

My mom was a bit worried about Pascal: guys his age had a one-track mind. But if sex was all Pascal thought about, I had no problem with that.

I'd usually go over to his place after school. He lived in the Basin with his father, in an apartment above a convenience store, the kind where the clerk sold hash under the counter. Pascal said you could buy a five-dollar ball of hash at the same time as your six-pack. His dad, of course, was no Alcan executive. My mom never wanted to drive me to Pascal's place, so I'd take the bus. I had to transfer to a second bus at the station on Racine Street, and when my mom found out, she changed her mind about driving me. No way did she want me down at the bus station. Dealers hung out there. They'd go back and forth between the station and Galaxy Arcade to sell mesc, hash and acid to the skids playing Duck Hunt and Contra all day long.

At Pascal's, me and him would lock ourselves in his room. I never met his mom, and I never knew if he saw her much. I didn't ask. I didn't want to piss him off with too many questions, but I think Pascal didn't give a rat's ass about his mom. He never mentioned her, except for one time when he said she'd bought him the tiger comforter on his bed.

Pascal's dad never once knocked on the bedroom door to see what we were up to all afternoon. The first few times there, nothing much happened. I was ashamed of my bras. Vanessa and Sarah were too flat-chested to lend me theirs, and anyways they didn't wear the kind of bra I wanted. I'd seen a type I liked in the window of La Senza, a bra that gave you cleavage like in the Chantelle ads. It came in red or black. I swiped one of each on the Thursday after our movie date. It was easy. There were two salesladies and the store was jam-packed. I slipped the bras into my knapsack and then walked toward the exit, my mind on something else so I wouldn't look nervous. At night in bed, I realized I should've swiped matching panties too. I'd seen in the porno videos that my dad hid in the suspended ceiling of our basement that the girls always wore matching panties. Garter belts were also good. Guys seemed to go wild over them, and I thought they were really pretty. I went back to the store to steal black and red panties not long after the bras, but there was only the large size left. Pascal didn't really notice the difference, though.

I hid the bras and panties in my knapsack before heading over to Pascal's. If my mom found them, she'd have a fit. She was always telling me that colored lingerie was for whores, even though she had plenty herself. I knew because I'd snooped in her underwear drawer. I'd also found a kind of naughty figure-skater outfit with frills and crotchless panties. I'd been amazed because my mom had always told my dad she'd rather die than wear a G-string. She probably had another man in her life. My dad had better not find out, because if he knew she had a boyfriend, he'd want to see me even less.

One afternoon at Pascal's, I looked at his alarm clock and realized we only had an hour left before his dad got home from work. I told Pascal to wait a sec and then shut myself in the bathroom and slipped on my red lingerie. I looked really good even though the panties puffed out at the back. I kept staring at my stomach and telling myself I had a nicer body than Melanie's. I was as pretty as the girl in the Budweiser poster in Pascal's room. I looked just like her except for the hair. Pascal seemed to think so too when I went back to his bedroom. I straddled his lap just as he was about to get up. *Dookie* was playing on the stereo, and he'd dimmed the light. He got a boner in his jeans, and I wondered why he wasn't making a move yet. I kissed him. He could touch me, I said. He started undoing my bra. I was embarrassed to show him my breasts. He started humping me a bit and heavy-breathing on my neck. Did I want to? he asked. I wasn't sure if he meant going all the way, but I said I didn't mind. He stretched out an arm to get condoms from his bedside table. I was freezing, and my high beams were on. The condoms glowed in the dark. I must've made a face because he said Melanie had bought them as a joke, but they were all he had left. I didn't care. I decided it was time to unbutton his jeans. Should he put on

38

another CD? he asked. I was tired of him stalling, so I started to jerk him off like in my dad's porn. After like five minutes, he moved my hand away because I was hurting him a bit, so I decided to give him a blow job. He sat on the edge of his bed, and when I started, he immediately put his hands on my head. The taste wasn't as bad as I'd expected, but I couldn't do much because his penis was too big and I couldn't fit the whole thing in my mouth. I tried awhile, but I gagged. Then I developed a kind of technique where I sucked just the tip and stroked the shaft. He didn't last two minutes. He shot up from the bed and then came all over his throw rug. I was super happy because it meant I looked pretty in my lingerie. I promised myself that next time I'd wear a garter belt.

After that day, I had like a new power over Pascal. He always wanted to be with me, and he'd bring me to the hole and the skatepark at the bottom of Racine Street. I couldn't invite Vanessa and Sarah, though. Pascal said they were prisses. Anyhow, I wasn't seeing them as much, and it was true they were prissy. They were scared of everything, and they were always lecturing. They said Pascal was too old for me. They thought he was a cheat due to the whole Melanie situation. A guy who ditched one girl for another couldn't be trusted. He was sure to dump me as soon as he met somebody prettier. I told them to shut the fuck up. They knew zip about guys.

All Vanessa and Sarah wanted to do was drink their SunnyD-vodka mix. They never wanted to go anywhere but the mall, which was fucking boring after a while. I felt like hanging out at cabins in the woods and places with no security guards around. Vanessa was terrified of going in the woods with guys she didn't know, and Sarah said her mom claimed that any girl who'd hang out in the woods was a whore. Vanessa and Sarah wouldn't even venture to the skatepark because kids did tons of drugs there and they were anti-drugs.

I could go in the woods with Pascal, so I didn't need my friends. Our favorite spot was the hole, which was in a little forest between Lower Vanier and Upper Vanier. You got there by the trail behind the convenience store. From below, you could also take the path alongside the baseball field, but I never went that way because you needed to climb the rock face and I was afraid of falling like my friend Louis, who'd broken both legs there. Anyways, the bus would drop us off just in front of the convenience store in Upper Vanier. The guys would buy beer, and I'd fill a small paper bag with sour watermelon candy, and then we'd head down. At the hole, we'd gather spruce branches and douse them with propane to make a campfire. Lots of kids from Falardeau, Canton and St. Honoré would come by to hang out. Almost all the dirt-bike trails led to the hole, and sometimes the skids would show up on their bikes and another fight would break out with Pascal and his buddies.

Kevin Bouchard was always at the hole with his boom box, and he'd play the Ramones and the Clash. I thought it was weird that Pascal hung around with him. Kevin didn't dress like us, but I liked his style. He wore a black leather jacket and Converse sneakers and combed his hair in a pompadour like in *Grease*. He was tall, lanky and pale, and he didn't talk much, except about music. Sometimes I'd bring my GrimSkunk and Propagandhi CDs, and Kevin would let me play them. Not too often, though. He was a total control freak who'd mostly only play his own stuff, always some obscure band nobody knew, like Operation Ivy. He'd make mixtapes but refused to copy them for us. I remember we'd all get ticked off about that. One weekend, this girl from Valin brought Green Day, and Kevin gave her a condescending look and told her to go play those poseurs and sellouts someplace else. The girl took off all humiliated and likely went and slit her wrists or something. Kevin was a goddamn maniac with his music.

I met Eve Côté at the hole. She lived in a big house on the bank of the Saguenay River. Eve was a year older than me and went out with Fred. I was impressed to meet her because she was like the most popular girl at school. She was really pretty with hair down to her butt and a mouth shaped like a heart. She even sang in an all-girls group that covered songs by Hole and the Runaways. I would've killed my own mother to play any instrument in that group, even something wimpy like the tambourine. Before I started high school, I'd already heard of Eve Côté. Her brother and three of his buddies had died when an Alcan train had plowed into their car at a railroad crossing. At the time, the newspaper said the traffic lights weren't working right, but some people claimed that the guys had made a suicide pact and driven onto the tracks. Eve introduced me to the girls who hung out at the hole. They were like the prettiest group of girls ever and had the coolest clothes. Melissa wore these crazy eighteen-hole Docs, which she likely bought in Quebec City. Two really cute twins, Isabelle and Annie Imbault, were also part of their clique. Rumor had it they took baths together, and the guys practically drooled imagining the scene. I forget the names of the others, but I know that one girl lived with a foster family and skated like a boy. They were always together, those girls, and at school everybody's eyes were drawn to them. They reminded me of fireflies.

One night at the hole, Simon and Melanie rode up on dirt bikes with a twelve-pack. Pascal went over to high-five Simon, and Melanie came and gave me a peck on the cheek like we were super close. She was probably acting all friendly because Eve was there. They'd been really tight when Melanie was going out with Pascal. Eve told me they'd stopped hanging around after Melanie claimed she'd left Pascal for Simon. Eve knew it was a big fat lie. It was Pascal who'd broken up with Melanie because he had a crush on me. He'd told Fred, who'd told Eve. Pascal was the reason why Melanie was always scowling at me and starting trouble at the mall, the cunt.

Anyways, that night we all sat around the campfire. It was freezing out, so cold it could've snowed. The weatherman had said we'd get ground frost, and I was sure my dad would forget to bring in his tomato plants. Melanie passed around cans of beer. I thought beer tasted nasty, so I gave mine to Kevin. He said I could put on my Bad Religion CD if I wanted. Melanie fished some mesc out of her purse. She told me it was the real deal this time and apologized again for her trick at McDonald's.

Simon was a dealer, and his mesc was cut at .5. I didn't know what that meant, but it sounded good. I said I wanted to try it. It was ten bucks a gram. Pascal bought me some, and I emptied half the baggie on my student card. Me and Eve made lines with my healthcare card. I hadn't poured the mesc on my healthcare card because it had indented letters and the mesc would've gotten stuck in the indents and been wasted. I thought I was a fucking Einstein for realizing that.

Eve told me to do just one line at first so I wouldn't get too stoned. I figured I was a pro, so I snorted two jumbo-size lines.

Within ten minutes, my head was spinning and my mouth had gone numb. Apparently I kept repeating myself, asking again and again what time the last bus went by the convenience store. Near the end of the night, Eve said I was a moron and that I should've listened to her and done only one line. I laughed and we went to dance near Kevin's boom box. I was still all stressed out about the bus, but I remember that some endless Sex Pistols song was playing on and on. Louis was bombed out of his skull. He was always getting the most twisted ideas into his head, and this time he started tossing empty beer bottles down the rock face. The bottles landed on the lawns and in the swimming pools of the people who lived next to the baseball field. They must've called the police because the cops drove up on their four-wheelers. They put out the campfire with bags of sand and emptied out any beers that were still left.

When they heard the cops coming, the guys from St. Honoré ran to their dirt bikes and zoomed off down the trail. Only two cops showed up, so they didn't give chase. While the St. Honoré guys were scrambling to get away, Simon had time to dump his mesc on the ground. The cops who searched us said they knew the drugs had been in Simon's pocket. They'd come to put out our campfire every Friday since the summer began, and they looked majorly fed up, like they couldn't wait for winter so we'd hang out someplace else. They knew Simon because they'd already arrested him with hash and acid at the bus station. Simon now had a juvenile record and couldn't get caught dealing again or else he'd be sent back to the St. George Institute. He'd spent the summer in juvie after the judge ordered him into rehab and group therapy. But that night, those two cops couldn't do a damn thing except call him a little bastard.

When the cops came to question me, I saw that one of them was a redhead. A carrot-top cop—man, how lame. His partner, though, was much scarier and didn't look like he'd just graduated from the police academy. He searched through my purse and found a rolled-up five-dollar bill and a plastic baggie. I started crying and couldn't remember my address. I was terrified the cops would call my parents, but they didn't phone anybody. Before they got back on their four-wheelers, they told us they'd return in an hour and by then we'd better be back home with our mommies.

CHRISTIANE F. was sleeping with Detlev, and I wanted to sleep with Pascal. First, I had to go on the pill, and I just assumed a doctor would ask for my mom's permission since I was only fourteen. On Sunday afternoons, me and my mom would often read together in the living room. I'd sit in the big La-Z-Boy by the window, and my mom would spread out on the couch with her pile of magazines and her wool blanket. It was fun because we'd make tea and dunk in our shortbread cookies. My mom had been given a box of green tea at her new job, and we were dying to try it since we loved anything Chinese. Too bad her green tea tasted like the cardboard box it came in. We dumped it down the sink and made our usual Salada with milk.

For two weeks, I'd been working up the nerve to talk to my mom. It was now time. She seemed in a good mood and hadn't brought up my dad all day. She'd finally stopped reading *The Manipulators Among Us* and just started *The American Black Bear: Prince of Darkness*. What was weird about her new book was it didn't even mention black bears, but I wasn't sure what the hell it was actually about. There was something cultish about

45

it. As for me, I was at the part of *Christiane F.* where she goes to a disco called Sound for the first time. My mom went off to the bathroom and when she came back, I ran through my spiel that lots of girls at my school were on the pill and maybe I should be too. It'd make me regular and cure my cramps. Well, my mom got all cranked up. Who did I think I was fooling? She wasn't an idiot. She wasn't born yesterday. She went to send my dad a fax. My parents were only in touch by fax because otherwise they'd get into fights.

On Halloween, two weeks earlier, somebody had buzzed our door at about four-thirty in the afternoon. It seemed a little early for trick-or-treaters. I grabbed a handful of candies and went to the door expecting to see our neighbor and her three-year-old kid, but it was my dad, who asked where my mom was without even bothering to say hello. Somebody must've died, I thought. My mom was on the phone with God knows who. I asked if my dad wanted to come in, but he shook his head. We stood in the doorway barely speaking for like five or ten minutes—the longest minutes of my life—and I didn't get why he wasn't asking about school, which was basically his only topic of conversation with me. Anyways, my mom finally got off the damn phone and dragged herself over with a big sigh to find out what my dad wanted.

Ever since the divorce, my parents had been arguing over who got what. My mom had been bugging my dad for these soapstone Eskimo sculptures they'd bought. And that afternoon, my dad had come for his Supertramp LP.

My mom wouldn't give it back. It was hers, she insisted. She'd bought it at the Supertramp show in Quebec City in 1976.

Roger Hodgson had invited my mom and a friend of hers to the band's trailer after the encore. My mom was always telling me this story. My mom refused to go in the trailer, but her girlfriend went, and apparently Roger and Rick Davies groped her big-time. My mom's friend came out with her skirt all crooked, her blouse buttoned up wrong, and a bloody nose.

I knew my mom would tell me this story just to scare me. She'd claim that even guys who looked pretty harmless could be closet rapists. If ever I got the urge to sleep with a boy, I just had to remember how Supertramp had messed with her girlfriend.

Anyways, my dad was furious that my mom wouldn't hand over the Supertramp record. He was talking really loud in the hallway, saying my mom was a fucking liar and that he was the one who'd gone to the Supertramp show. He was like that, my dad. He'd make up stuff and believe his own lies. He'd never been to a rock show in his life, but he swore he'd gone to Quebec City in 1976. My dad pushed my mom aside and came in. He picked up the cordless phone on the kitchen counter and said my mom should call his brother Jimmy if she didn't believe him. He'd gone to the show with Jimmy, he said. We all knew my uncle had been dead for three years. My mom called my dad a jerk, and he stomped out of the condo, leaving the door wide open. My mom could shove that fucking album up her ass, he yelled back. He'd buy the CD, and it'd sound tons better than her crappy LP. Well, my mom was so enraged by my dad's antics that she got the Supertramp record and followed my dad out to his truck. He was already backing down the driveway and spinning his wheels, so she flung the album at his pickup. She came back in, cursing and calling my dad a psycho.

Later, after she shut herself in her bedroom, I went outside to get the record. It was covered in snow, so I brought it in, wiped it off with a dishtowel, and slid it back into the album rack in the living room. I thought my mom would eventually come out to make dinner. The doorbell kept ringing, and after two or three trick-or-treaters, I didn't feel like handing out candy anymore. I took down the decorations on our front door, switched off all the lights, and shut the drapes in the living room. It seemed my mom wouldn't be making us a meal after all, so I sat slumped on the couch with the bowl of candy in my lap. *Friday the 13th* was on TV. It was the scene where a camp counselor gets her throat slashed in the woods, and I was so terrified I pulled my mom's blanket up to hide my eyes. I felt like turning the lights back on and changing channels, but at the same time I sort of liked being scared, so I stuck it out till the end.

After the movie, I went straight to bed but couldn't fall asleep. I was paranoid that Jason was in my closet or under my bed. I glanced at my clock radio, and it was exactly midnight. I was even more petrified because it was the witching hour when Bloody Mary would appear. I'd better not look in the mirror opposite my bed. I said Bloody Mary in my head. I didn't want to see her, but I couldn't help chanting Bloody Mary, Bloody Mary. Suddenly there was a loud crash. My heart stopped. Was Bloody Mary smacking the walls? Would she appear before me with her white rags and zombie face? I scrambled out of bed to go wake my mom. As I went by my mirror, I shut my eyes. I stepped into the hall at the same time as my mom, who'd heard the noise too. I was freaking out. It was cold, and there was a draft coming from somewhere. I grabbed my mom's hand, and we crept down the hall. We had no idea what was going on and couldn't see much except for a big white light shining at the other end of the apartment. When we reached the living room, I realized it was cold because the bay window had shattered into a thousand pieces. We recognized my dad's truck on the hill across from our place. My mom's biggest soapstone statue—a bear—was in the middle of the living room lying among the shards of glass and candy wrappers. My mom picked up the bear. It was as hard as a rock, that damn thing. I saw my dad stumbling around the front yard without his coat and gloves on. The door to his pickup was open, and Supertramp was playing in the background, the song that goes, "Mummy dear, mummy dear." Snowflakes were drifting through the broken window, and my mom was totally speechless. After that episode, my parents started communicating only by fax. The lawyers said it was better that way, and things did calm down.

On the Sunday when I asked my mom about the pill, my dad stopped by the condo after dinner to have a talk with me. Why did I want to go on the pill? he asked. That crap was for whores. The three of us were sitting around the kitchen table. My mom had served my dad a Grand Marnier and given me a glass of juice. All my friends were on the pill, I told them, and it'd make me regular and stop my awful cramps. My mom said I should just take two extra-strength Tylenols for my cramps. Only easy girls took the pill at fourteen, she insisted, and if I went on it, the boys at school would find out and think I was a tramp. My dad laid it on extra thick by saying that guys didn't marry those kinds of girls. I didn't care one bit. Eve was on the pill, and all the guys were crazy about her.

The next day, my mom drove me to the clinic to get a prescription for birth control. We went to the one in Jonquière because she knew a nurse at the Chicoutimi clinic. In the car, she said not to breathe a word to my dad. My mom probably decided that taking the pill wasn't as bad as getting pregnant. She likely mulled over the question all night and then called her friend Sandra in the morning. Sandra would've told her the pill was a smart move. She was cool. Plus, she'd had a kid at fourteen, so she knew what she was talking about.

The doctor praised my mom for bringing me to the clinic. He said I should wait thirty days before having sexual intercourse. When he said "sexual intercourse," I cracked up. My mom gave me a stern look and said I was being immature.

On the way back from Jonquière, we stopped for a coffee at the Croissant Café. My mom would take me there whenever she had something serious to discuss. These mother-daughter talks were likely recommended in the three hundred books on raising teenagers that she read while I was off at the mall in the evenings. On account of those books, she was always talking about quality time and stuff like that. The last one she bought, *The Lobster Complex*, basically said that teens were ungrateful snots who'd build a shell around themselves. I remember I thought that comparing teenagers to lobsters was the most retarded thing in the world.

Since I didn't drink coffee, I ordered some juice. College students were studying at tables all around the coffee shop. We chose a table near the window even though a half-finished soup and a used coffee mug were still there. They took forever to clear the tables at that place, and it always bugged me. My mom moved the soup and mug to another table and wiped our table with one of the napkins she always kept in her purse. She took a gulp of her coffee as she watched people going by outside. This time, she didn't beat around the bush for five minutes like she usually did. Instead, she looked me straight in the eye and said there was no way I was going to sleep with Pascal. I reassured her I had no plans to sleep with him right away. That seemed to calm her down. Afterward, we talked about her new hair color and how fun it'd be to go to Florida during spring break. My mom said we'd rent the condo of one of her aunts, who lived half the year in Fort Lauderdale. I asked if the condo was near the Salvador Dali Museum, but my mom didn't know where that was. My art teacher had told me the name of the city, but I'd forgotten it. The name sounded like a town in Russia or something. My mom said she'd ask her aunt's husband, who was an anesthesiologist and would probably know.

Later, we stopped at the Jean Coutu Pharmacy nearby to pick up my pills. The next day, I started marking Xs on the calendar in my agenda. I wondered how I could steal a garter belt over the next thirty days. I couldn't go back to La Senza because the saleslady had given me a dirty look the last time. She suspected something for sure, and my dad would kill me if I got busted shoplifting. I rummaged through my mom's underwear drawer in case she'd bought a garter belt, but I only found the figure-skater costume. Where had the crotchless panties gone? Maybe she'd left them at her boyfriend's place. She'd admitted to me the night before that she'd started dating a guy three days after we'd moved into the condo. No surprise there: my mom hadn't been single for more than ten minutes since the day of her first period.

By November 12th, there was already a foot of snow on the ground. The guys at the hole had decided to build a cabin in the woods so we'd have a place to hang out in the winter. Kevin's dad was lending them a hand. He worked in construction and gave them old building supplies instead of dropping the stuff off at the dump at night. Pascal went around bragging that our cabin would be the biggest in Chicoutimi. They'd even insulate it for the winter because Kevin's dad had a deal on mineral wool at Potvin & Bouchard Hardware.

The most amazing part of the cabin would be the mezzanine, which would have old single mattresses spread out on the floor to sleep on. Plus, we'd have a potbelly stove to heat the place. Kevin's mom would donate two old couches that were just sitting in their basement, and we'd put them on either side of the stove. We'd also bring a table for playing crazy eights and asshole, as well as a boom box for dancing. It was Kevin's idea to have dancing because otherwise girls wouldn't come.

The police didn't want teenagers putting up cabins in the woods, but we didn't give a flying fuck. You couldn't walk more than an hour into the forest without coming across a cabin. Kids from Chicoutimi and Chicoutimi North were all building cabins to spend their weekends in. The cabins were like our parents' cottages on the Valin Mountains, but not as swanky and way more fun. Like the cops, a lot of parents were dead set against the cabins. They suspected their kids would get into all kinds of mischief—drinking, drugs, sex—and even claimed that some younger girls had been gangbanged in a cabin. As for my mom, her big fear was fires. The summer before, half the woods behind Valin Falls burned down due to some careless teens, and the houses nearby almost went up in flames too. But we weren't nimrods like those kids, and besides, Kevin's dad had given us tips on preventing forest fires. Anyhow, all kinds of dicey things were rumored to be going on at the cabins, so Chicoutimi's mayor decided to ban them. That was why Kevin, his dad, and the other guys were building our cabin at the very end of Chicoutimi North, near St. Honoré. It was a damn good idea because the provincial police controlled that sector. They had only two cop cars to patrol two hundred kilometers, and a gang of Satan's Guards and other sleazebags in the area kept them pretty busy. Those cops had way better things to do than hassle teenagers in the woods.

In late November, we put the finishing touches on our cabin. One night, we threw a housewarming party, but for our friends only because we didn't want some bigmouth blabbing where our cabin was. There were bastards who'd trash a cabin just for fun, so Kevin warned us to keep quiet about ours.

We weren't scared to take the trail to our cabin in the daytime, but at night with a flashlight, it was like *The Evil Dead*. Whenever I took that trail, I'd think of the scene where the demon trees

53

rape that girl. So on the night of the housewarming, me and Eve didn't want to walk up to the cabin on our own. We insisted a guy wait for us at the entrance to the trail.

Simon said he'd be there around seven-thirty. When we arrived, Melanie wasn't with him, but Pascal and Kevin were. I remember we thought it was so adorable that the guys had come as a group. We had to laugh because we were sure they were just as scared as us to walk alone in the dark.

It was a half-hour trek from the road to the cabin, but we could already hear music after we reached the stream. Kevin had made a special mixtape for the party, and a Stray Cats song was playing in the distance. He'd started a rockabilly phase a few weeks earlier and was wearing tight jeans and a Cramps T-shirt. I remember that on the trail I thought he looked really cute and I wanted to kiss him.

At first, the other guys would call Kevin a fag on account of his tight jeans. Us girls, though, all said he looked hot, and we'd started adopting a rocker look ourselves after our first few times at the hole. Then the guys finally caved in too, even though they never wore jeans as skintight as Kevin's. As for me, I kept my Docs but also wore lots of leopard skin and had my hair in a French twist. I thought Christiane F. dressed that way, and I wanted high-heel boots like David Bowie wore. Kevin thought I looked really pretty as a rocker. He told me so the night of the party while Pascal was doing hot knives on the mezzanine with a guy from Valin. Me and Kevin were sitting on the plaid couch beside the wood stove, and my thighs were practically on fire because it was so hot. Kevin was rooting through his knapsack for a CD. His look was like something straight out of a movie. It was insane. He could've been in black and white, and nobody would've batted an eye. Plus, I'd never seen a knapsack done up so beautifully. It was a Lavoie knapsack like the ones we all had. We'd cover them in liquid paper, writing names of bands or drawing marijuana leaves. Isabelle had even copied the lyrics of a Runaways song on hers. But, man, Kevin's knapsack was a real work of art. Drawn on the back were three covers of Bowie albums—Bowie's best work, according to Kevin. The liquid paper must've taken four days to dry. On the front, he'd written KURT COBAIN IS NOT DEAD, 1967–1994 in like fifty-eight different ways. I was sure he could've sold his bag for three hundred bucks at Planet Rock. Kevin was tired of looking for his CD, so he turned his whole knapsack upside down. Out fell a dozen mixtapes, a live CD of the Stooges in Berlin and other groups I liked, a flashlight, a book about the Stones, a cigarette lighter, and a journal with pictures of bands and a photo of a dog glued to it. Was the dog his? I asked. He nodded and passed me his journal so I could see the dog better. He picked up one of the CDs and then stuffed everything back in his bag. I asked what kind of dog it was. A Wheaten terrier. His parents had bought it from a breeder in Ontario. It was a rare breed apparently, and its mother had won lots of blue ribbons at dog shows. I thought dog shows were so gay. I'd once heard Brigitte Bardot on TV saying they were even a form of animal cruelty, but I didn't mention this because Kevin had just given me a compliment. I wanted to be nice to him, but I'd felt all funny when he said I was pretty. He'd hardly ever spoken to me before that night. I gave him his journal back, and he went to put on "(She's) Sexy + 17."

Eve got up from the other couch and started dancing. Melissa, Annie and Isabelle joined her. Melissa looked like a bit of a spaz,

Annie and Isabelle danced pretty good with their twin-sister moves meant to attract looks from the guys, and Eve shook her butt in a way her dad wouldn't have approved of. I went to dance with her and tried imitating her moves.

I was sure I looked like a moron, but I wondered if Kevin was watching me or the Imbault twins. When "Search and Destroy" came on, I was so hot I decided to take a breather outside.

I didn't bring my coat, and it was freezing out. It was kind of dangerous around our cabin because the ground was so slippery. The night was moonless and pitch-black, so I couldn't see a damn thing and I knew that under the snow lurked old boards with rusty nails sticking out. My mom was always saying rusty nails could give you tetanus. I almost stepped on one as I walked over to the big boulder lying behind our cabin.

I sat on that boulder for like ten minutes. I had goose bumps but didn't want to go back inside right away. It was too hot in there, and I was feeling all awkward due to what Kevin had said earlier. I was hoping Pascal would come out, but he was probably lying stoned on a mattress with his blowtorch because he never showed up.

Eve opened the door to the cabin and yelled "Catherine!" a couple times, but I didn't answer. Nine Inch Nails was on. She went back inside. I was sitting on my hands so I wouldn't get my skirt dirty, and soon I heard the music play louder as the door to the cabin opened again and slammed shut. I thought Eve was coming to stalk me, but it turned out to be Kevin, with his flashlight and my coat in his hands.

He climbed on the boulder to sit beside me. I was glad because I was getting fucking cold. We soon decided to move down to the stream to get out of the wind. I held on to branches and the trunks of dead spruce trees lying in the forest as we made our way down. Kevin walked ahead with his flashlight. The light created a kind of white cone, and we could see tree stumps that the wind had uprooted and knocked over. The forest cracked and swayed, and I kept imagining wolves and bears everywhere. Kevin said he'd never seen a girl so scared of tree stumps. When we came to the stream, we sat on a spruce trunk. I didn't want to get my skirt all sticky, but I realized it'd be fine because the sap was probably frozen. The stream was freezing over. I could see the water flowing beneath the thin crust of ice, and it made me thirsty.

Kevin took some mesc out of his jacket. He gave me a rolled-up bill, and I snorted right from the baggie. I did more than usual since his mesc wasn't as good as Simon's. It came from the Valin dude, who'd owed Kevin money and paid him back with mesc. He was a slacker who was always broke and bumming beer and smokes off everybody. For some reason, Kevin told us to give the guy a break. It wasn't his fault. The poor guy had had a shitty life. Kevin snorted the rest of the baggie, and I said we should head back before Pascal came looking for me. Kevin straightened the collar of my coat, staring at me with a sort of dazed smile. My heart was thump-thumping. I'd never noticed what perfect teeth he had. He'd worn braces for sure. He took my hand to help me up, and then we stumbled back to the cabin. Because of the snow, I almost fell once, but Kevin caught me in time.

When we came into the cabin, Pascal had his coat on and was bent down tying his boots. He stood up and looked pretty wasted. Where had I been all this time? he asked. Kevin quickly hung up his jacket on the back of the door with the other coats and then went to change the music. The Imbault sisters yelled to put on Depeche Mode, and Melissa clapped her hands. I told Pascal I'd gone to sit on the boulder out back because I was feeling queasy. I didn't mention the stream. Pascal had been looking for me because he wanted to make out up on the mezzanine. He let me climb the ladder first, and I saw Eve, Fred and Simon on a mattress together. Eve was in her bra and had bigger boobs than I'd expected. Her boyfriend was unbuttoning her jeans, and Simon was trying to undo her bra. I wondered where the hell Melanie was.

Me and Pascal lay down on a mattress at the very back. Did I want to go all the way? he whispered. The thirty days weren't up yet, so I said no. He didn't seem too peeved, but he started deep-kissing me straightaway. I liked it once I began pretending he was Kevin. Downstairs, a trippy song was playing, but I didn't know what it was.

After a little while, Pascal actually nodded off. He'd always crash whenever he drank too much beer and smoked up. He could fall asleep any old place and any which way. I wondered how he could sleep with the music blaring and the girls shrieking downstairs.

Pascal's mouth was wide open, and he was blowing his pot breath in my face. It was gross, so I turned over. Not far from us, Eve, Fred and Simon were going at it hot and heavy. Eve was stark naked, and Fred was licking between her legs. She was wriggling, and Simon was watching them. At one point, he began staring at me and jerking off. I was mortified. I turned over and pretended to sleep. I waited like fifteen minutes and then turned back over to check if Simon was still looking. No, he was sucking Fred off. Eve was lying beside them, dead to the world. I was sure the two guys weren't gay, just really, really wasted, but the more I watched them, the more I thought Simon was totally into it. He must've been a closet case.

I woke up on the mattress just as it was starting to get light out. Music was still playing but not as loud as the night before. It was probably six or seven o'clock. I couldn't check because I'd left my watch in my purse. Kids were curled up in their sleeping bags on all the mattresses. Downstairs, the guys were still playing quarters. I could hear a quarter spinning on the table and the guys laughing. I got up and climbed down the ladder, trying not to wake Pascal and the others.

I had a throbbing head and cotton mouth. Kevin was sleeping on a couch with his knapsack as a pillow and his two hands under his cheek. He looked eight years old. When I brushed by to get my purse, he grabbed my hand and pulled me toward him. He kept his eyes closed the whole time, so maybe he was only half-conscious or at least faking it. We spooned for like five or ten minutes even though he smelled like booze when he breathed down my neck.

I finally got up from the couch and opened the window in the front door to air the place out. The cabin reeked of stale smoke and alcohol. A girl I didn't know who was sleeping nearby on the couch grumbled that it was fucking cold. I left the window open anyway and just threw her a coat to use as a blanket. Simon came down in his boxers and a hooded sweatshirt. I asked where Melanie was. On vacation with her folks in Cancún or Caracas, he couldn't remember which. That made no sense because I thought her parents were on welfare, but whatever. Simon frowned at the Valin dude and Fred, who were still playing quarters. He told them to clear off the fucking table because it was time for breakfast for chrissake. Then he went outside on the porch in his socks to pee in the snow. He left the door wide open, and I hurried over to close it. I hadn't realized Simon was so grumpy in the morning. The other guys went out to pee with him.

It was starting to snow. When Simon came in, he rummaged around for the bread that Eve had brought. We'd make toast. He asked if I knew how to build a fire. My dad had shown me how, so I dressed warm and went to gather small branches and birch bark, which we kept underneath the cabin. I thought the clearing near the boulder would be perfect for a campfire. I lit the bark and added dry wood, but my fire wouldn't catch because these gigantic snowflakes kept snuffing it out. I had to restart it three times. Simon came out to join me. We speared slices of bread on the end of a branch, and I toasted them. When we went back inside, we realized nobody had brought anything to spread on the bread and we had nothing to drink. Me and Simon tromped down to the stream with our cold toast in our hands. Simon tapped holes in the ice with his boots, and I slurped up like a gallon of water and then got scared I'd get the runs. My mom had always warned me to drink only tap water when out camping.

I told Simon I had a wicked headache. He took a joint out of his shirt pocket and said smoking up would help. I took two puffs and right away felt nauseous. I barfed on the edge of the stream, and Simon laughed at me. After he finished his joint, we went back inside. The girl was still sleeping under the coat, but Kevin and the others were awake and had flopped on the couches. Fred was complaining that the Satan's Guards were selling him mesc cut at .20. They were screwing him over, and he was pissed. They'd never sell him pure PCP, he said, because then he'd make his own mesc. To buy the real deal, he'd need to cross the wildlife reserve since the Guards' territory ended at the village of L'Étape.

Kevin got up to put on music. I didn't know the song playing but was positive it was David Bowie. I knew Christiane F. loved Bowie, and I knew she would've loved Kevin too. On the couch, Pascal kept running his fingers through my hair. I always sort of hated people playing with my hair, so I said to stop and he called me a whiner. I told him to screw off. Me and Eve got up and went out to wash our faces in the stream.

I felt like spending the rest of the day at the cabin and doing a bit more mesc. Anyhow, my mom wasn't expecting me. She was off at her new boyfriend's cottage for the weekend. She said that at fourteen I was able to look after myself and that if anything went wrong, I could just go to my dad's place. I was happy to be left alone and wouldn't be stopping by my dad's.

Eve had some mesc left over from the night before, and hers was way better than Kevin's. I snorted three or four lines, and Eve said I'd gone overboard. I started feeling super woozy. I said wow was her boyfriend ever open-minded. Was I a prude or what? she replied.

Pascal took off at like ten o'clock with the Imbault twins and the Valin dude because he had to go help his dad wash their pickup. The mesc had kicked in, so I wasn't sure if he'd even said good-bye before leaving. I just sat on the couch watching the snow fall and wondering what we'd eat for lunch. We didn't have much, but I remembered Kevin had Corn Pops. I knew that by lunchtime I wouldn't be super hungry, but we'd never have enough cereal for everybody. I suddenly had a thought: we could set rabbit traps. The night before, I'd seen a roll of copper wire hanging on a nail behind the stove. I mentioned my plan to Kevin, who thought it was a damn good idea.

Nobody else wanted to come. Eve laughed at me and Kevin and called us the Robinson Crusoes. We slipped on our coats and went out with a pair of long-nose pliers and the roll of wire. I wasn't actually sure how to snare rabbits, but Kevin would know.

We walked a little ways into the woods, looking for rabbit tracks. Kevin explained that we'd see them in the snow and should set up our snares in those areas. I was glad he knew how to hunt. When I was little, my dad always said real men could basically hunt any kind of animal. That way, if the end of the world came, they could still feed their families. Hunting rabbits was a good start.

After fifteen minutes, I was too fried to walk. I asked Kevin if we could sit down a bit. There was no place, though. He said I'd better sit on his lap so I wouldn't get hemorrhoids from the cold snow. Kevin sat cross-legged on the ground, and I sat on him. He still smelled like booze. He started stroking my hair and my cheek and told me I shouldn't have done so much mesc so early. I said nothing even though I didn't like him playing with my hair.

I stared into the woods. There were no dead branches lying in this area. At one point, Kevin said the forest looked beautiful and that his dog would love to be out running with us. He could help us catch rabbits. I wished I could pet his dog. I hated running, though.

Kevin asked if I'd ever done nexus. I knew it was a pill and a kind of speed, but I'd never taken it. He said he had some on him.

It'd probably cancel out the mesc a bit, he said, but he didn't look too sure. He took the pills out of his jacket pocket. I told him to zip up his jacket because it was winter, but he just wrapped his scarf around his neck and claimed he was immune to the cold. I didn't say anything. I totally knew he just didn't want to wreck his rock-star look even in the middle of the forest. We swallowed a pill each. Then we got up and went on our way. We must've set up five or six snares, but we didn't have any hunting tape to mark where they were. I don't remember if we even talked during all this.

When we got back to the cabin, everybody was freaking out. They'd been waiting for us for three goddamn hours. Well, Kevin had frostbite on his hands and feet, and I had hypothermia. At least, that was what they told us in the ER.

Eve was the one who insisted we go to the hospital. On TV, she'd seen mountain climbers who'd lost limbs from frostbite after attempting to climb Mount Everest. I had my stomach pumped in the ER. I prayed the whole time that I wouldn't puke because the nurse—this fast-talking lady who was only like four foot one—said we'd have to start all over again if I threw up. Afterward, she told me to stop filling my body with crap and to dress like a normal person when I went hiking in the woods. She didn't call my mom. She looked like she didn't give a shit. Anyways, my mom's boyfriend had no phone at his cottage.

My mom and dad were arguing about where I'd spend Christmas Eve, her place or his. Neither, I told my mom right off the bat. I'd go to Pascal's. She called me ungrateful and started in on her damn lobster kids again. On the phone, my dad said I could just stop by his place whenever I felt like it. I wouldn't feel like it and he knew it. I was sure he'd said so just to look good. He had a new girlfriend and was probably arranging to have her move in.

My mom was almost never at the condo. She'd spend all her time at her new boyfriend's. I'd invite Pascal over after school because I was sick of his place. His tiger blanket stank of cigarettes, and his dad never did much housework. I'd always leave there with itchy eyes and a runny nose. I was allergic to cats, and Pascal had two. Their fur was like halfway between long hair and short hair. Two black-and-white brothers. The neighbor's cat had had a litter of kittens, and Pascal and his dad had adopted the last two to keep them together. I'd always thought black-and-white cats were pretty low class. They were the type that shed constantly. Also, one of them was always peeing at the bottom of Pascal's closet. The whole apartment smelled like cat piss, which didn't seem to bother Pascal and his dad, but it grossed me out. Pascal would throw his clothes into his closet instead of hanging them up, so when he wanted to wear something, he'd need to smell it first to check for cat piss. Totally barf-inducing. I'd always been squeamish and hated anything to do with piss and shit, and that really bugged Pascal. He said I was such a snob and that I was turning into a priss like Vanessa and Sarah.

On the thirtieth day of being on the pill, I invited Pascal to our condo after school. I always got home around three-fifteen. I called my mom to see if I could expect her for dinner or if I had to thaw something out. She said she'd be sleeping over at her boyfriend's place, but she'd made me some macaroni. I just had to add a little water to moisten it and then zap it in the microwave.

I threw the macaroni in the dumpster behind our building. I didn't want my mom to know since she was always afraid I wasn't eating. Her books on teenagers claimed a poor appetite might be a sign of anorexia or, worse, drug addiction. Christiane F. barely ate. She wanted to squeeze into her tight jeans, and also heroin ruined her appetite. I hadn't been eating for a while, and I could fit into almost anything.

I often wondered if I had no appetite due to the mesc. All us girls on mesc were rake thin. Except Melanie. I never figured out why, with all the mesc she snorted, she still had her stripper belly. Pascal called it that. He said all strippers had a gut even if they were a perfect ten everywhere else.

Pascal buzzed our door around four o'clock. He didn't smell like cigarettes or cat piss, so it was a good start. He smelled like his dad's Drakkar Noir. We went in my room, and I put on some old Aerosmith. Not their crappy hits with the videos that played ten times a day on MuchMusic and starred those snotty cunts Liv Tyler and Alicia Silverstone. No, the good stuff that Kevin had on his mixtapes.

Pascal loathed Aerosmith. It was music for fags, he said, and he kept bugging me to put on Pennywise. I tried explaining that "Dream On" was one of the best songs ever, but he wouldn't listen, so I played his fucking pseudo-punk to make him happy and stop his bitching.

We were sitting on my bed, and I began kissing him. I remember he kept ramming his tongue into my mouth and twirling it around. Saliva grossed me out too. While we were making out, I kept thinking that I hadn't managed to steal a garter belt. Also, I was sure Kevin kissed way better than my boyfriend.

Pascal took off my sweater. He had trouble unhooking my bra because he was shaking like a leaf. I didn't understand why since he'd already gone all the way with Melanie. He shouldn't have been so jittery. Anyways, I undid my bra to help him and then unzipped his jeans. He was wearing boxers with the Batman logo on them, and I thought it was ultra dorky of him to pick those boxers for our first time. Of course, I'd never seen him in anything but uncool underwear. He had a Superman pair, a white pair with a hole in the butt, and a couple of faded black pairs.

I told Pascal I was ready. I'd put on clean sheets and turned the heat up to twenty-five so I wouldn't freeze like at his place. I'd stuck a Post-it beside the light switch as a reminder to turn the heat down later. Whenever I blasted the heat, my mom would go postal because our electricity bill might go up. I lay down on the bed, and Pascal climbed on top of me. I remember that he made these humping movements and was really heavy and, oh my God, I felt like laughing. Pascal asked if I knew how to put a condom on with my mouth. As if. He put it on himself while I waited. I looked away so he wouldn't feel self-conscious. He was wearing his hair in a messy bun with a pencil stuck through it, and I realized he didn't actually look much like Kurt Cobain.

Pascal climbed back on top of me and tried pushing his penis in, but he wasn't able to. He fumbled around for like ten minutes. He had a huge dick, and it really hurt. He finally got off me, and we cuddled under my comforter. It wasn't working because I was nervous, he said. I probably wasn't ready. I was a lot younger than him. It was normal. He understood these things. He told me I shouldn't worry or be embarrassed and that if I wanted, he could do other stuff to me.

Pascal went down on me, and I think I came. I'd never come before, even when I'd touch myself in my room at night while pretending to make love to a cross between Pascal, Kevin and Detlev. What I'd do to myself felt good, though, especially ever since I'd discovered my mom's vibrator and started swiping it when she was at her boyfriend's. Yet those times weren't as intense as when Pascal ate me out. I wanted him to do it again right away, but he wasn't much into it. He told me so afterward, right before he asked me to return the favor.

I didn't get what Pascal meant at first. Then he took my hand and put it on his penis. I jerked him off, and he came on his belly. It took a real long time, and God was my wrist ever sore.

I remembered the mescaline I had in my purse. Pascal thought I was crazy: you didn't do mesc at six on a Wednesday night. I couldn't care less what he thought. I got out my leftover mesc and made myself a big fat line on his Pennywise CD. Pascal got in a snit. The PCP would wreck the CD sleeve, he whined. I called him a douche bag. As if my mesc would fuck up his damn CD sleeve.

I switched on the TV, and *Mrs. Doubtfire* was on. I was feeling all spaced out, like when we'd gone to see *Seven* at the movie theater at the mall. Pascal had been forced to explain the story to me the whole time because I couldn't follow a thing. But his explanations weren't much help because I split before the end to do more mesc in the restroom with Eve. After the movie, Pascal and Fred went looking for us all over the mall. They even headed down near Canadian Tire, but me and Eve had decided to walk to the skatepark to see Kevin and buy some acid.

As for *Mrs. Doubtfire*, I couldn't make heads or tails of it. I was super whacked out and started channel surfing. Pascal was getting hungry, and I was sorry I'd thrown the macaroni out. We looked in the fridge, but there wasn't much except hot dogs and buns. We rolled the hot dogs in paper towels, nuked them in the microwave, and then sat down with them in front of the TV. Pascal asked if he could smoke some hash. Yeah, he could as long as he used a Bounce blower. To make one, I got an empty toilet roll out of the wastepaper basket in the bathroom and stuck a Bounce sheet at one end. I needed an elastic to hold it on, but I couldn't find one anywhere. We could just use string or something like that instead, so we hunted through the kitchen drawers and finally found some butcher's twine. We attached the Bounce to the toilet roll, and then Pascal toked up. It smelled like fabric softener all over the condo.

Instead of eating my hot dogs, I gave them to Pascal because he was getting the munchies. He didn't care I wasn't eating, and maybe he didn't even notice.

We tried to fuck again around ten, but it still wouldn't work. While we were trying, Pascal's father called to tell him to come home since it was a school night. My mom phoned to check on me not long after Pascal took off. She said my voice sounded funny. It was because I was reading, I lied. She wanted to know which book. *Christiane F.* My mom told me not to stay up too late. I did my last line of mesc and lay in bed watching MuchMusic. This blond airhead was droning on about No Doubt. I can't remember her name, but she was wearing denim overalls.

During a commercial, I phoned Eve to tell her about my fiasco with Pascal. Her first time had been weird too. If Pascal got all nervous, it was bound to be horrible, she said. We'd just have to practice. It'd go okay the next time.

We talked about Melanie too. She'd broken up with Simon. I thought it was because he'd had a threesome with Eve and Fred at the cabin. Fred had bragged to one of his buddies, and everybody at school now knew. Eve didn't give a damn. Melanie wouldn't dare lay a hand on her.

Eve said she was worried about Fred because he hadn't called her in like three days. He'd driven to Quebec City with some bums from Jonquière to buy PCP. He was through with the bikers and wanted to start selling more mesc. One of the Jonquière dudes knew a punk who hung out at D'Youville Square. The punk apparently had the best PCP in Quebec City, but he was homeless and hard to track down. He usually lived under a viaduct with his dog but moved around a lot to dodge the cops. Fred was probably looking for him. At worst, he was partying in Quebec City with the Jonquière guys. It was possible. He'd done it before.

I WANTED TO DYE my hair black, but my mom said no. I didn't understand why. She'd been dyeing her own hair blond since she was like thirteen. My grandma would buy her the dye and color my mom's hair for her. My mom had told me so a million times. She'd always use Nice 'n Easy No. 101, Natural Baby Blond. She'd ditched the drugstore dye when she'd met my dad. Only trailer trash used dye from a box, and no way would I be putting that crap in my hair.

The first Saturday of every month, my mom would go see her hairdresser, Denis. His salon was in Jonquière, and like all male hairdressers he was a fag. I loved going there with her. The receptionist would always tell me I was beautiful and let me paint my nails. I'd sit under the big hairdryers with a pile of fashion magazines and look for Calvin Klein ads with photos of Kate Moss. I'd seen on *Flash* that she had a heroin habit and was dating Johnny Depp. On the cover of her book, Christiane F. looked a little like Kate. The same eyes and hair at least. Kate was prettier, though, probably due to the foundation they slathered all over her face.

My mom had once explained to me that the girls in fashion magazines had their makeup done with special cosmetics, not the crappy stuff you bought from the lady behind the counter at Sears.

Years ago, my mom had done a photo shoot in her bikini in L.A. I think it was for Hawaiian Tropic tanning oil. When she was on the set, she noticed a big pimple on the side of her butt. She tried adjusting her bikini bottom to hide it, but the makeup artist spotted the zit and told my mom not to panic. The woman went into the trailer and came out with this little bottle of foundation. As she was unscrewing the top, she said the foundation cost five hundred bucks. She dabbed some on my mom's zit, and the thing vanished. Kate's makeup artists had the same kind of magic potions, I was sure, because no girl looked that good naturally.

Denis was blathering on about the hair shows he'd be attending in New York and London. Whenever he went, he'd win some big prize. That was why my mom and all the other snobby ladies from Arvida and Chicoutimi wanted him to do their hair. You had to book an appointment like three months in advance. And he took the summer off because the hair shows were held then.

I didn't get why Denis had his salon in a hellhole like Jonquière if he was such hot shit. My mom said he was just really, really in love with the region. I had my doubts, though, that he actually won medals at those hair shows. My guess was that he closed shop in the summer to take a break from the broads at his salon and to travel with his twinkie boyfriend, who was a stewardess or whatever you call a guy who does that job.

That Saturday, I didn't want to go to the salon with my

mom. I was sulking because she wouldn't let me dye my hair black. While she was getting ready in the bathroom, I snorted two lines of mesc in my room. Once she was gone, my plan was to meet up with Eve and Melanie and then go to the mall and swipe earrings from Ardene. Afterward, we could head to the cabin to see the guys. They always threw a party on Saturday night, and I was in the mood to go.

My mom knocked on my door and then barged in before I could answer. I barely had time to hide my baggie, student card, and rolled-up bill under my pillow. My nostrils were all red, my mom said. She thought I'd caught a cold at school because a bug was going around. I said I didn't feel sick and then faked a little phlegmy cough. My mom went to get the Buckley's Syrup. From the bathroom, she yelled that she could lend me some of her fifty-dollar face powder to hide the red. I said okay, so she applied some to my nostrils, but it wasn't the right shade since my skin is super pale like my dad's. My mom took out her concealer and told me it'd do the trick. You had to choose a concealer a shade lighter than your skin tone. She'd taught me that when I was like four years old. I looked at myself in the little mirror in her compact and thought that the five-hundred-dollar foundation would've done a better job. My nostrils were still all red, but according to my mom the concealer had made a world of difference.

My mom absolutely insisted I go with her to the salon. I could hang out at the mall another time. She'd even drop me off at the entrance to the trail to our cabin in the late afternoon. We could pick up Eve and Melanie on the way. My mom must've been feeling high herself because she'd never give me a lift anywhere but to Pascal's. I wondered what the hell was up.

73

In the car, I sniffed the whole way. I was tripping out and scared my mom would think I was acting weird. When we got to the salon, I asked to wait in the car. Not a chance. She hadn't raised a hick. Did I want people thinking I was uncivilized? Anyhow, she was only getting a trim today, so the appointment wouldn't take long.

I walked into the salon looking all sulky but trying to act normal. The receptionist gave a little shriek when she saw me and then came over and handed me a cape. Her and my mom kept exchanging looks and laughing. Denis hurried over and announced that today was the big day.

My mom said she didn't want me coloring my hair with the junk sold at the drugstore. That stuff was full of aluminum and supposedly caused cancer. Denis would do my color. I just had to explain to him what I wanted. No fucking way. My mom was seriously awesome. I planted three or four kisses on her cheeks and then plunked myself down in Denis's chair.

I wanted jet-black hair with a blue sheen like Mia Wallace had. I'd rented *Pulp Fiction* the week before and really loved her look. I asked my mom if Denis could cut my hair the same way. Yeah, he could. Denis hadn't seen *Pulp Fiction*, so I got a pile of magazines and leafed through. I found Mia's bob in the magazine that was named after the Madonna song. That hairstyle was all the rage, Denis told me. Lots of girls in London had bobs. My mom was thrilled and so was I, but I had trouble pretending I wasn't strung out.

It took two hours for Denis to turn me into Mia Wallace. When he finished drying my hair, I looked in the big mirror and flipped out. I'd never been as beautiful in my entire life. I could pass for eighteen. Eve would freak over how pretty I looked. Pascal would too. He was always saying how much he liked girls with black hair. He'd called them Pocahontas. Well, with my porcelain skin, I didn't look much like an Indian, but still.

On the way back to Chicoutimi, my mom said she had another surprise for me. Since I'd be spending Christmas Eve with Pascal and she'd be at her boyfriend's cottage, she might as well give me the present now. Anyways, Christmas was right around the corner.

Her present was hidden in an old unwrapped box at the top of her bedroom closet. My mom handed me the box. The whole time I was tugging the tape off the top, she had tears in her eyes. She looked so sweet, but I didn't tell her that.

Inside the box was a pair of snakeskin cowboy boots. My mom had had them since the age of seventeen. These were the boots she'd worn to the Supertramp concert and plenty of other shows too. I'd need to take good care of them. She said to apply Vaseline using cotton balls and wipe in the direction of the scales. She'd had them resoled, but snakeskin was fragile, so I couldn't walk in water or slush. If I wanted to wear them at the cabin, I could as long as I carried them there in a plastic bag and put them on once I got inside. Anyhow, it was winter and those boots didn't look too warm. My mom always bought me winter boots that were toasty warm but butt-ugly. I was amazed my mom had given me her snakeskin boots.

Around six o'clock, my mom dropped me and Eve off at the entrance to the trail. We didn't know where Melanie was. She hadn't been calling either of us very often lately.

I'd decided to wear tight black jeans, a big white collared

shirt of my mom's, and a red bandana around my neck to look even more like Mia Wallace. Eve was in her leopard-print blouse and this pencil skirt that was totally smoking. As we headed up the trail, I carried the snakeskin boots in a bag, but I put them on before we reached the cabin so I wouldn't look like a dork changing my boots in front of everybody. They wouldn't get wet because Ski-Doos had packed down the snow on the trail.

When we were halfway there, we saw a partridge perched in a spruce tree. It was staring right at us. I told Eve that a partridge was so stupid you could kill it just by startling the thing. My dad had taught me that when we were out hunting small game. Anyways, I yelled my head off, but the partridge barely blinked. Eve screamed with laughter. Then she picked up a big rock from the edge of the trail and hurled it right at the partridge. The bird fell on its back and started wriggling around. Eve didn't know what to do next, so I chucked another rock at it and right away the partridge stopped moving. I remember that blood trickled out of its beak and spread across the snow.

We decided to bring the dead bird to the cabin since the guys would know how to prepare it. When we arrived, I left it just outside the front door so it'd freeze. We could pluck its feathers the next day. We went inside, and the place was pretty crowded because Fred was back from Quebec City with his PCP. He was up on the mezzanine cutting it.

Kevin didn't say a word when he saw me with my new black bob. He kept glancing over at me, though. I asked the guys where Pascal was. Upstairs with Fred and Melanie. I started climbing the ladder but didn't get halfway up before Fred's panicky face appeared over the ledge. He told me to stop right there and began climbing down to block my way. I told him to move his ass or I'd knock him off that ladder. He looked down at me and said if I really wanted to see my boyfriend screwing Melanie, that was my problem. I heard Melanie whispering loud over the music, and she was in a fucking tizzy. Fred hung off the side of the ladder and then dropped to the floor. I wanted to see that fat cow's face, so I climbed up. By the time I stepped onto the mezzanine, they had most of their clothes on. Melanie was staring at the floor, but I could see tears in her eyes. Pascal started making excuses straight away. He was drunk, he was stoned, she threw herself at him, it wasn't his fault, sex with me wasn't working, he was horny. Pascal yammered on and on, but I stopped listening. I wondered how the hell my boyfriend could cheat on me with that skank. And why wouldn't his dick fit inside me anyway? Was I some freak of nature? Finally, I called Melanie a slut bucket and then climbed back down.

Downstairs, everybody knew what had just happened and was looking at me weird. Was I okay? Eve asked. I was fine, but I was now dying to try Fred's new mesc. Simon threw some wood in the stove, and then Melanie came down the ladder. Nobody would look at her. As she walked by the stove, Simon spit on her and ordered her to get the fuck out now. I think it was at that exact moment I became queen. I'd suddenly turned into the goddess of fireflies.

Everybody on the couches acted like nothing was wrong and just kept talking about the No Use for a Name show in La Baie. Fred was sitting at the table and preparing lines. To cheer me up, he said I'd be the first to try the mesc from Quebec City. It was special mesc that he'd cut at .4. It was just for us. No way could he sell any at the bus station or Galaxy Arcade. If word got out that this excellent shit was floating around town, the bikers would be breathing down his neck. If ever they turned up at his house, his parents would ship him off to the St. George Institute for the rest of his life. Fred asked if I had a bill to snort with, and I took a ten out of my purse. He told me to promise I'd snort no more than two lines over the next three hours because otherwise I'd get way too blitzed. I said okay, okay, and then went to sit beside Kevin on one of the couches. The Pascal situation was like total bullshit, he said. He was worried about me. Did I want to go for another hike? We could talk. The stream was likely frozen over by now, and we could skate on it in our boots. I wanted to stay inside and see what would happen when Pascal came down from the mezzanine. I wasn't too shook up, really. I just felt like hanging with Kevin and never ever thinking about Pascal again. Fred gave us his spot at the table, and I snorted two lines like Fred had said. I left only one line for Kevin because he was sort of delicate.

I was in the mood to dance. I pulled Eve up from the couch, and we started doing the moves the guys always went wild over. Kevin put on "Girl, You'll Be a Woman Soon" and I began dancing just like Mia Wallace. He played it for that reason, I was sure. As for Eve, she was imitating John Travolta and cracking up. I knew that all the guys in the place were watching me and that the girls would start talking about me behind my back. I didn't give a fuck. I was the goddess of fireflies. I'd do what I wanted.

I can't remember if Kevin put the song on repeat, but he probably didn't. It always ticked him off when some dolt played the same song ten times in a row. Anyways, I must've been really whacked because that song lasted for a goddamn hour. At one point, Kevin came to dance with me. He put his hands on my hips. He danced really good. He was like in the same league as Patrick Swayze from *Dirty Dancing*. I was so hot I unbuttoned my shirt all the way. Simon was always cramming the stove with wood. We'd told him a thousand times to add only one log at a time, but it apparently never sank in.

I danced in my bra with my shirt open, and I couldn't care less if people saw my tits. "Rock 'n' Roll Suicide" came on, and Kevin kissed my neck. Right after, I heard a girl in a corner yelling and saw Pascal slam his fist into the wall. He stormed out of the cabin in just his T-shirt and sneakers. The guy from Valin took off after him with Pascal's coat in his hands and a hat that was maybe not even Pascal's. The Valin dude never caught up, though, and soon came back inside because it was too frigging cold out.

I remember that when we were dancing together, Kevin had a hand on my neck and I could see a yellow light radiating from my body. He kissed me, and then all I could hear was David Bowie. We were at Sound. I was wearing a black leather miniskirt and making up all kinds of dances. My mom was marrying the King. My dad was showing me how to gut a moose. I was drawing a map of the world. Eve was sprouting hair like Rapunzel's. I was canning rainbow trout. Kevin was merging with the light. Outside the partridge had frozen solid. It was fucking useless to us now.

My mom changed her mind about Christmas. She found out I'd broken up with Pascal, and she didn't want me staying all alone in town even though I promised to drop by my dad's place on Christmas Eve. I was in no mood to head up to the cottage with my mom and her boyfriend. Paul got on my nerves big-time. He was so tacky with his Polaris shirts and his sweatpants. Plus, whenever we ate dinner together, he'd always be after me to finish my plate. It was majorly annoying because I was never hungry and food would practically make me gag.

My mom said I absolutely had to go to the cottage—end of story—but I could bring a friend along so it'd be less boring for me. Eve was the only person I felt like inviting. My mom would never let me bring Kevin. Besides, I didn't even know if we were going out. I'd only seen him one other time at the cabin, and tons of people were around. I acted like nothing had happened, and so did he, I think. Maybe he really wasn't into me. Or maybe he was afraid of Pascal. Probably not, though, because Kevin never let anybody push him around. Anyways, it looked like Pascal and Melanie had hooked up again. They were always together at school, but they kept out of our way. They'd better or we'd tell them to fuck off.

My mom called Eve's mother to see if she minded if her daughter spent Christmas with us. I didn't hear much of what they said because my mom shut herself in her room with the phone. She kept her voice down, but I did hear her say she'd watch us like a hawk.

Eventually she passed me to Eve, who was all gung ho about going to the cottage. Christmas had been a downer at her house ever since her brother's accident. In the woods, she could go snowmobiling and snowshoeing and wouldn't have to deal with her dad moping over the photo album of her dead brother. Plus, the forecast was for sunny skies.

We left for the cottage the morning of the 24th. My mom's boyfriend was in a good mood because it'd snowed all night, but that didn't stop him from complaining that we had too much luggage. I was sure I'd have fun with Eve even if it meant putting up with my mom and Paul. We'd brought four grams of Fred's mesc. My mom wouldn't notice if we snorted some. She didn't even know what the hell mescaline was.

To get up to the cottage, we had to drive in the pickup along a logging road for an hour. I was always scared to death because that road was narrow and we'd pass logging trucks on their way down. Their trailers would often skid, so we had to be careful around the bends. A couple from Long Lake had died at kilometer 33 the winter before. A trailer had swerved right into them as they went around a bend. The paper said they'd been killed instantly. Whenever I'd see a logging truck in the distance, I was petrified I was about to die.

After the logging road, we'd stop to register at the gateway. We called it the gateway, but it was basically just a cottage. The couple in charge of the gateway lived there year-round like hermits. The man—Bernard was his name—looked after the local Ski-Doo trails all winter long. His wife, a lady named Diane, registered people and sold gas to guys with Ski-Doos. In the summer, she'd weigh the trout that fishermen would bring back down, and she'd make sure the rack of Yum Yum vinegar chips was always full. Bernard also worked as a fishing guide for the tourists from France who rented cottages.

People had to register at the gateway whenever they entered the controlled area. The purpose was to monitor hunting and fishing, but also to record how many people went up and note the date they planned to come back down. If some guy didn't return when he was supposed to, Bernard would trek up and check on him.

Having to register pissed everybody off royally. In the woods, we wanted to be left in peace. They were the only place where city laws didn't apply. For example, people would crack open a beer and drive with the bottle between their legs as soon as the road going up turned to gravel, after Falardeau.

Paul hated registering too. Whenever Diane asked him to fill out the form, he'd insult the government and wildlife officials and call them Big Brother. Registering, though, had actually saved the life of a guy named Mr. Bourassa. I think it happened in the fall. Mr. Bourassa didn't come back from his cottage on the Sunday like he usually did. In the late afternoon, Bernard decided to go check on him before dark. He found Mr. Bourassa in bed. The guy had carbon monoxide poisoning and hadn't even woken up that morning. Bernard called Airmedic on his ham radio, and Mr. Bourassa was lifted out of there in a helicopter. At the hospital, the doctor said if Bernard had arrived fifteen minutes later, Mr. Bourassa would've been a goner. Instead, the guy became a vegetable. I didn't see how being a vegetable was better than being dead. I mean, Mr. Bourassa now crapped his pants and couldn't even go back up in the woods.

Anyways, my mom's boyfriend kept his Ski-Doos in one of the sheds behind the cottage at the gateway. Everybody had Ski-Doos and stored them in the sheds. It was way easier than bringing them from home in the back of a pickup with all the luggage the women dragged up.

While Paul was getting the Ski-Doos ready and gassing them up, my mom chatted with Diane. She asked for the woman's pâté recipe, but Diane wouldn't share it with just anybody. My mom hadn't won her over yet and would need to keep coming up to the cottage for a couple years to get that recipe.

We'd gone inside so my mom could register and also so that me and Eve could slip into our snowmobile suits and our furry boots. Those boots were the only things that kept your feet warm in the woods, my mom said. She'd lent a pair to Eve, but she'd bought me some new ones. They were really nice, my two-tone, cow-fur boots, but I didn't tell my mom. She'd be way too pleased with herself and use it against me later.

When he finished loading the sled with all our luggage, Paul came inside to tell my mom I'd need to carry a plastic crate the whole way up to his cottage. We put our things in crates so they wouldn't break or get covered in snow. We had forty-five minutes of snowmobiling to do on a trail as wide as St. Genevieve

Boulevard before we reached Paul's cottage. The sled was jam-packed because my mom had brought too much stuff. Eve would sit behind Paul on one Ski-Doo, and me and the extra crate would be stuck behind my mom on the other.

On the way up, Paul zoomed along the trail so fast we had trouble keeping up around the bends. I was scared the whole time that I'd fall off because I had to hold on to the damn crate instead of hanging on properly.

When we arrived, my mom asked me and Eve to fetch wood out of the shed to heat up the cottage. It was about fifteen below out, so we had to hurry if we wanted the place to be warm by lunchtime. Paul went down to the lake to get some water. The hole had frozen over during the week. The temperature must've dropped to more than twenty-five below for sure. He'd need to break the ice with an ax. The hole never froze unless it was really fucking cold out.

Paul took the ax and buckets out of the shed and tossed them onto the sled. The lake was about two hundred feet from the cottage, at the bottom of a little hill, but it was better to take the Ski-Doo. Afterward, he could bring all six buckets of water back to the cottage at the same time.

Six big buckets was what normal people would need to spend a week in the woods, but since my mom was with us, Paul would have to drive back down to the lake a dozen times during our holiday to fill the buckets. At the start of the winter, she'd given her new boyfriend an ultimatum: if she couldn't bathe, she wouldn't be going to his cottage. She'd wash herself with just a facecloth for no more than two days. After that, she insisted on a bath or a shower.

Her boyfriend had set up a tub-shower in the extension on the cottage. He ran a pipe down to the lake to draw water up with a boat pump. So my mom could have hot water, he installed a propane water heater just above the shower. When the lake froze over in late November and we couldn't use the boat pump anymore, Paul would hook the water heater up to a big green garbage can. He'd pour four buckets of water into it, and my mom would have hot water for five minutes max.

At first, people in the area would laugh at my mom and her tub-shower. City slicker was what they called her. But soon the ladies in the nearby cottages started whining for a tub-shower too, so all the men had to install one or else their wives would stay back in town. My mom had even invited women whose husbands were too wimpy to install a tub-shower to come bathe at Paul's place. Nobody dared laugh at her after that.

Paul seemed really nuts about my mom even though they hadn't been going out very long. Plus, he was good with his hands. My dad was an expert at building things too. He could rip out and redo a bathroom in a single weekend. I didn't know what he'd think of my mom's tub-shower, though. He'd likely examine it a couple minutes so he could find some flaw and call Paul a screw-up. Then he'd tell Paul how he would've rigged up something better. My dad was the type who thought he was superior to every other man on earth. Anyways, I wasn't even sure he knew my mom had a boyfriend. I hadn't spoken to my dad much since our talk about the pill because he was too busy with his new girlfriend.

My dad had met someone not long after the divorce. My mom even thought he was going out with her before. He claimed he'd met her in a support group for divorced people. I didn't buy that story. No way in hell would my dad join a support group. The one time he'd stepped foot in an AA meeting, it was to check who the alcoholics were in town so he could blackmail them if they ever crossed him in court.

I'd met my dad's girlfriend in the front yard of my old house while she was helping him rake up dead leaves. She wasn't nearly as pretty as my mom, but I had to admit she seemed nicer. My mom had never once helped my dad with the yard work, and she didn't even like me helping him. Why should we muck around in the dirt when plenty of people would kill to come work in our yard? My mom had always wanted my dad to hire a company to do landscaping around our house, but my dad refused. He might as well throw his money out the window, he said.

My dad's girlfriend had tried being friendly with me that time in the yard. I'd taken the bus there to mooch twenty bucks off my dad to buy some mesc. He had no cash on him, so his girlfriend gave me a twenty. I remember I wanted to give her a compliment to thank her, but I kind of choked in the middle of my sentence. I told her that her highlights looked awesome, but she should dye her gray roots because they gave away her age. My dad called me a smartass, but his girlfriend said it didn't matter. She was actually pretty decent.

At the cottage, me and Eve went inside first with the logs and kindling. It smelled nasty in there. I yelled about the smell to my mom, who was outside connecting the propane behind the cottage. Eve discovered a pile of shit in the bathtub. My mom came inside to see at the same time her boyfriend arrived with the buckets. He said a marten must've weaseled its way into the cottage and taken a dump in my mom's tub. When animals got scared, that was what they did. Shit, I mean. We never did find where that marten had slipped in, though.

My mom washed the bath with bleach, and then we lit the wood-burning stove. It'd take two or three hours to heat up the cottage, and due to the marten situation, we had lunch later than usual. My mom made minestrone soup and a platter of raw vegetables. I hated raw vegetables, so did Eve, but we ate them anyway.

After lunch, my mom put the meat pies near the wood stove to thaw. She'd prepared our Christmas Eve dinner in town during the week, which was why we had extra crates with us. She'd also made a sandwich loaf, a fancier version covered with Philadelphia Cream Cheese instead of Cheez Whiz. My mom had made everything in advance so she could go snowmobiling with Paul in the afternoon, but first we had to cut down a Christmas tree in the woods nearby. Few fir trees grew that high up, so we settled for a black spruce, which we decorated with silver tinsel and red balls. We didn't have a nativity scene or even a star to go on top. In the woods, you had to make do with less, Paul said. My mom laid our presents under the tree and then asked if me and Eve wanted to go snowmobiling with them. We'd stay behind and listen to our music, I said. My mom didn't mind.

Her and her boyfriend would return before sundown. They'd go all the way to the outfitter on Pepper Lake before turning back. That gave me and Eve two full hours alone. We started the generator, switched on the stereo, and put on a crappy Guns N' Roses album. We liked listening to *Use Your Illusion I* in secret, especially tacky songs like "November Rain" and "Don't Cry."

We'd put them on repeat and act out the video where Stephanie Seymour marries Axl Rose. We'd later learn that he slapped her around all the time, although to me she didn't look like the battered-wife type.

Eve asked if I'd ever sniffed gas. Never. Only Indians and lowlifes were gas sniffers. She said no, no, it'd be fun and the high would fade fast. I said I was game then. We dressed warm and went out to the shed to find a canister of gas. There was an old five-gallon canister with gas at the bottom. Eve went first. She screwed off the cap and inhaled three or four times, and then she stumbled out of the shed, staggered around, and fell on her butt in the snow. I sniffed a few times too and tried to get out of the shed, but the door seemed to be swinging in all directions. Outside, the trees were whirling and my ears were ringing. I went to sit down next to Eve, but I brushed against her by accident and knocked her wool cap off. We laughed and stared at the sun like total morons. The buzz was way too strong, and I couldn't wait for it to wear off. It took five minutes max for the trees to stop their swaying. Afterward, we headed back inside to snort some mesc instead. We decided that gas sniffing really was for Indians and lowlifes after all.

We didn't put any music on because I wasn't allowed to run the Delco too long. It wasted gas, Paul had warned us. We snorted our lines in the living room on the coffee table with the Mod Podge top. If we each did just one line of Fred's mesc, we thought we'd be okay by the time my mom got back.

But no, we were still blitzed when we saw the lights of the Ski-Doos coming over the lake. It was starting to get dark out and must've been like four-thirty. When my mom came in, we pretended to be playing asshole, but I couldn't hold my cards straight. I kept dropping them, and Eve would giggle. My mom went to check if we'd raided the liquor cabinet, but none of the bottles had been touched. Eve asked my mom if she needed help with our dinner. I kept asking what we were having. Meat pies. My mom had already told me at lunchtime.

My mom put the pies in the propane oven to heat up and then asked Eve to make a lettuce salad with a cream dressing. As Eve was taking the iceberg lettuce out of the fridge, she dropped it and the lettuce rolled under the counter. She should just rinse it with the spring water from our jug, my mom said.

Meanwhile, I was reading *The Vampire Lestat*. I was so wasted I'd started the same page like twenty times. Eve cut herself with a fillet knife while making the salad. She was bleeding a lot, and I kept asking my mom if we had to go to the hospital and if we could still have dinner anyway. My mom asked if we'd taken anything. No, of course not. No way. She ordered us to open our overnight bags and empty our pockets.

When she found the mesc in my makeup kit, my mom turned as white as a sheet. Her boyfriend was steaming mad and called us little shits. My mom wanted to know what the hell that crap was and who'd sold it to us. Eve said an older girl had given her the mescaline, but she swore she'd never done any before and that we'd just wanted to try it. I told my mom we were sorry we had. We hadn't realized it was so strong. We'd only smoked pot one time and hadn't even liked it. She could flush that mescaline down the toilet because we never wanted to touch that stuff again. We were way too scared and figured you could probably even OD on mesc. My mom said she wouldn't tell Eve's mother or my dad if we promised never to touch that crap again. We gave our word, and then she threw the rest of the mesc in the wood stove. God, I almost wept.

Paul said my mom was being a pushover. If it was up to him, he'd book us a room at the Institute. Plus, that damn powder wasn't mescaline. No way no how, he said. His brother had seen real mescaline in Mexico. It was made out of cactuses, and hippies took it to see their animal totem. The stuff we snorted was some chemical shit. My mom cut him off: the St. George Institute was a place for delinquents, and anyway it was none of his business. It was dinnertime, and she didn't want to hear another word about mescaline. She didn't want my stupid antics ruining Christmas.

Me and Eve covered the table with the Christmassy plastic tablecloth that my mom had picked up at Dollarama. Then we laid out the forks and knives in their proper places to please my mom. We ate our meat pies drowned in ketchup even though we felt like puking. I even had some salad and a slice of sandwich loaf to make my mom happy. I was scared she'd change her mind and tell my dad she'd caught me with drugs. If so, he'd throttle me for sure.

Around midnight, we opened our presents. Paul had bought my mom a swanky Polaris snowmobile jacket. I got a Discman to replace the one that Melanie had thrown in the toilet, a hundred-dollar gift certificate for clothes at Jacob, and the novel *The Queen of the Damned*. I loved stories about vampires, and so did Eve. She asked if I'd lend her the book after I finished it. I told her she'd have it in no time because I read super fast. Our school librarian had even said so.

After unwrapping our gifts, we hit the sack. My mom didn't wish me good night before she headed to her room, and in fact she barely looked at me. Me and Eve went to brush our teeth. She filled a Styrofoam cup with water from the lake, and I told her to throw it down the sink and take some spring water instead to avoid getting stomach flu.

We slept in the bedroom next to the living room. It had bunk beds, but Eve didn't want to sleep on the top bunk all alone. She was afraid of the dark, and even of wolves, although Paul had explained that wolves had died out on the mountains back in the seventies.

Anyways, I climbed up to sleep beside Eve. She was rummaging through her overnight bag for her PJs. She gave me a sneaky grin, pulled out three baggies of mesc, and wagged them in front of my face. The girl was a fucking genius. The mesc had been in a secret pocket that my mom hadn't noticed. We turned on a flashlight, and Eve whispered that it'd be cool to get high before we went to sleep.

We snorted almost a gram each. I wasn't too stoned, though. Eve started trashing Melanie and said she didn't get why Pascal had taken that cuntface back. I was so over that whole episode. All I cared about was whether me and Kevin were really going out. Eve thought we were. Kevin was totally in love with me. It showed. Everybody knew it, she said, and all the girls at our cabin were jealous because they wanted Pascal and Kevin and I'd gone out with them both. It was because I was really pretty, she thought, especially with my awesome haircut.

While she was talking, she started rubbing my back over my pajama top. It felt kind of good. I'd always liked backrubs. When I was little, my dad would often rub my back, and my mom would get all jealous because he'd never rub hers. My dad would snap that she wasn't five years old and to get over it already. Usually when he talked to her like that, my mom would take off shopping for hours. I'd stay behind with him, and he'd put on a movie and rub my back the whole way through. And my mom would come home with a surprise for me from the mall—My Little Pony, a Barbie, a diary.

About an hour into my backrub, Eve started giving me little kisses on my neck and then slid her hand underneath my pajama top. I didn't know what to do. I'd never been so embarrassed in my life. I thought if I moved over in bed, she'd stop. At the same time, I didn't want to hurt her feelings. I didn't think Eve was a lesbian. I mean, she was seeing Fred and was like a total guy magnet. Eve must've felt I was freaking because she whispered to me to chill, that we were just having a little fun. I told her I'd never done anything with another girl. I wasn't sure I'd like it. She kissed me on the mouth a bit. It wasn't too gross, so we started making out. I could feel myself getting wet. In my head, I kept repeating that I wasn't a dyke, that it was just for sex.

I started touching Eve's breasts. I remember they were heavy and bigger than mine and that I kept stroking them. At one point, Eve pushed my hands away and then slid down under the covers. She slipped off my panties and left them bunched up somewhere at the end of the bed. She went down on me a real long time. It was even better than with Pascal because she also slid her fingers in. I didn't know where she'd learned that technique, but my legs were trembling and I wanted to cry out. I held back, though, because I would've woken my mom and her boyfriend and caused an even bigger drama.

The next day at breakfast, I felt so awkward. I barely looked at Eve even when she was talking to me. She acted like nothing had happened. I thought my hands still smelled like sex, and I was flipping out. I wanted to go back home and hide in my room forever. I was convinced that the whole school would find out and I'd be a reject till the day I died. And I was sure Kevin wouldn't want me as his girlfriend anymore.

In the afternoon, Eve said it'd be fun to make a snowman since it was mild enough out for good packing snow. My mom gave us an old scarf and a carrot for the nose. We started rolling a ball of snow just in front of the cottage. Paul was chopping wood next to the shed, and we kept laughing at him because whenever he'd swing his ax, he'd make a face like he was taking a shit.

After the snowman, we thought it'd be cool to build a snow fort like we used to do as little kids. We started digging a tunnel in the snow, and an hour later it was longer than the front porch. My mom told us to be careful because the fort could cave in on us. We might suffocate like the St. Bernard in the movie *The Dog Who Stopped the War*.

We spent the rest of the afternoon in our fort talking and looking through the hole in the tunnel at the magpies. They'd come to peck at the leftovers from our dinner scattered in the snow near the door to the cottage. My mom would always give them table scraps because she thought the magpies had nothing to eat in the winter. Everybody in the area fed them, and they'd fly from cottage to cottage all day long. What they really loved was bacon fat. Paul would empty the fat into an aluminum pie plate and leave it on the porch. Even before the fat congealed, the magpies would swoop down. We'd also pour any kind of leftover fat into a Mason jar. When the jar was full, we'd cut a length of rope and dip one end into the fat. We'd leave the jar in a snowbank for the fat to freeze, and then we'd break the jar and hang the block of fat above the big doors to the shed. Paul liked watching the magpies fight over the fat while he was putzing around in the shed in the afternoon. The birds would turn into little butterballs and also get really, really tame. I didn't understand why my mom let us feed the magpies. My dad had always said it was wrong to feed wild animals. They'd become dependent on us and wouldn't learn to find their own food.

In the fort, I'd almost forgotten about the night before. Me and Eve were lying on our backs and scraping the ceiling of the fort so little snowflakes would float down on us. Eve was talking about her brother. Three months before he died, he'd started saving up to buy a Ski-Doo. He'd spotted a new MXZ at Villeneuve Equipment. All the guys bought secondhand snowmobiles from classified ads. He would've been the first in his circle to get a brand new machine. It really sucked that he never got a chance to buy the thing. Eve went quiet awhile and just kept scratching at the ceiling. The sun was setting, and the light was fading in our cave. I said we should go back inside. Eve said she hoped I wasn't all hung up about the night before. I asked if she was in love with me and told her I was in love with Kevin. Well, she laughed her head off for like ten minutes. I was so adorable, she said. Of course, she wasn't a lesbian. She just sometimes slept with her best friends for a kick. If I was too much of a square, we never had to do it again, and that would be that. I said no, no, I was super open-minded, and she said good. I realized she'd likely slept with that bitch Melanie and her fat belly. I turned to

Eve and said it'd be wild to do some mesc right there and then in our fort. She took a baggie out of the pocket of her snowsuit. Damn, that girl was prepared. We snorted that mesc like there was no tomorrow. All of it. For old, stale mesc, it was still really kick-ass. I could barely focus on Eve's face, and I didn't know if it was now dark because it was past six or because we were having a bad trip. I got paranoid that we were using up all the oxygen in the fort. We'd already been in there for like two hours, I thought. I was sure we were poisoning ourselves with our own carbon monoxide like I'd learned in science class. I told Eve we had to get out right that minute. She said I was a dork and almost kicked me in the face as she was crawling out of the tunnel.

Outside, it wasn't as dark as I'd expected, but the Big Dipper was already visible in the sky. I pointed it out to teach Eve where it was. In the woods, you could use constellations to get your bearings. She just needed to remember that Paul's cottage was right underneath the Big Dipper and she'd never lose her way. I was a total retard, Eve said. That constellation was Ursa Major, not the Big Dipper, and everybody knew that.

My mom came out on the porch as we were arguing and asked what the hell we were yelling about. I told her we'd used up all the oxygen in the fort and had almost died from carbon monoxide. My mom told us to stay put, that she'd be back in two minutes, and we didn't have time to think before she hurried back out in her snowmobile suit with three helmets in her hands. When she came up to us, she looked furious. She shoved the helmets onto our heads so hard I had a sore neck the next day. She knew what to do with smartasses like us. If we couldn't breathe right, it was on account of the crap we'd taken.

Well, she'd put some fresh air in our goddamn lungs and bring us back down to earth. Eve looked at me like she didn't know what was going on. My mom revved up her boyfriend's White Track because her snowmobile couldn't hold three people. She motioned for us to climb on behind her, and she yelled that we'd better keep our visors up the whole time or else she'd push us off the Ski-Doo. We'd go snowmobiling all night if necessary, and me and Eve would breathe deep and come down from our fucking high because if Paul figured out we were stoned again, he'd murder us both.

My mom squeezed the throttle, and we zoomed off toward the lake. After we drove onto the ice, my mom followed the marked trail, which was bordered by two rows of baby spruce and spanned the entire lake. I was sure we'd take the same route as usual, that we'd cross Long Lake, Round Lake and Pepper Lake and head along the trails that Paul and his buddies had opened up between the lakes. Well, I was dead wrong. My mom swerved off the normal trail at lightning speed. I was scared out of my wits. My dad had always said never ever to leave a marked trail, particularly on a lake ten kilometers long like that one. It was a matter of life or death, especially if it was snowing. I was afraid we'd meet the same fate as Mr. Leclerc and his wife.

That night, Mr. Leclerc's wife had been driving. She must've convinced her husband that he was too drunk and that it'd be better if she drove them home to their cottage. A storm was raging, and like an idiot she left the marked trail. In those conditions, everything would've looked the same—the sky, the ground, the shores of the lake. Apparently, she went around in circles for ages trying to find her way home, but the Ski-Doo ran out of gas at the far end of a bay. They both froze to death sitting on their snowmobile.

Our snowmobile was now tearing through two feet of powder snow, which was flying into my face and getting under my helmet. I couldn't see a thing, and my cheeks were freezing off my face. My mom was fucking livid. We were in serious trouble this time. Eve was grabbing on to me for dear life. We were coming to the end of the lake and must've been near the inlet, where there was practically no ice because of the current from the river flowing into the lake. My mom turned at the very last minute. She was a goddamn maniac. I was scared the Ski-Doo would flip and Eve would get crushed underneath. My mom drove along one of the biggest bays and then crossed the marked trail without easing up on the gas. My face was frostbitten for sure, and my nose would likely turn black and rot off. My mom seemed bent on hauling our asses all around the whole freaking night. I yanked my visor down to save my face and prayed it'd all end soon. Anyways, I sure wasn't stoned anymore, and Eve was about to break me in two from gripping me so hard.

By the time we got back, we were frozen stiff. After she slid off the Ski-Doo, my mom glared at us and said we'd lie to Paul that me and Eve had asked to go snowmobiling on the lake before dinner. We shuffled into the cottage and hung up our snowmobile suits behind the wood stove to dry. Voices were coming out of the ham radio, and Paul was snoring with his mouth open on the couch. A spaghetti sauce was still on the burner, and there was even garlic bread in aluminum foil on the counter. Eve asked my mom if she should get some 7 Up out of the coolers in the extension. The table was already set. My mom told us to sit down.

The next night, Paul showed us the photo album of his cottage. Me and Eve were bored out of our skulls, but we pretended to be interested because if we were nice enough, maybe my mom wouldn't rat us out to her mother and my dad about the mesc. In the middle of the album were photos of white and yellow lights. I asked Paul what they were. He didn't know, he said. He'd taken the shots in the late summer on his four-wheeler.

Paul told us he'd been coming back from Top Lake, where a buddy of his had a cottage. It must've been about one in the morning. He suddenly saw a big white light over his shoulder. It was too low to be the moon, so he stopped his vehicle to see where the light was coming from. The night was pitch-black, and this white glow hovered over him like a humongous flashlight. Paul said it'd stopped at the same time he had and then started following him again as soon as he drove off.

My mom told Paul to stop bullshitting us, and he swore on a stack of Bibles that he wasn't pulling our leg. He'd driven back to the spot the next night at the same time to snap pictures of the light. Eve was sure that it'd been a UFO. I agreed. My mom, though, figured that the army had been doing experiments with some top-secret equipment. After all, the army base wasn't too far away, so maybe they were doing tests like down in Area 51. Nope, Paul said, because the next night he'd seen more lights rising out of the lake in front of his cottage—yellow lights this time—and no way had some military equipment caused them. They weren't the northern lights either. He'd seen auroras dozens of times on the mountains, so he knew the difference. I wondered if the yellow lights were some giant species of firefly. It hadn't been firefly season, Paul said. The yellow lights had really come from the lake bottom, big rays of light that had risen through the water and drifted up into the sky. He couldn't swear that aliens had caused them, but he couldn't swear that they hadn't either.

WE CAME BACK FROM the cottage on the Sunday before school started up, around January 7th or 8th. On my mom's answering machine were three messages from Kevin and one from my dad. Kevin wanted to know if I was back in town. As for my dad, he hoped I'd had a good holiday. He wondered if I'd gotten the check and the card his secretary had sent me, and he asked when I'd start back at school. He suggested we go for brunch soon at the Deauville with his new girlfriend so he could introduce us officially. At the end of his message, he wished me a happy new year and complained that we didn't see each other enough.

That evening, I asked my mom if I could invite Kevin for dinner. I hadn't seen him over the holidays and felt like getting together, and besides, he'd never been to our place. Absolutely not, she said. We'd eat together just the two of us. In any case, I was grounded because I was on drugs. She wanted me to know how my life would play out over the next two months. She'd mulled the matter over at the cottage and decided to lay down some new rules. First, I'd hand over the check my dad had given me for Christmas because there was no way I'd get more money to buy more crap. Starting the next day, I'd come straight home from school. No goofing off. No dropping by Eve's house before dinner. I wasn't allowed out weekday nights or even on weekends. No hanging around the mall. And especially no parties at the cabin. And there was more. She'd search my room and go through my things at least once a week. She wouldn't tell me when, and it could be any hour of any day. If she found drugs or anything fishy, she'd ground me for two more months. She was tired of me jerking her around, so I'd better clean up my act and play by the rules. She even threatened to call Eve's mother about the mesc if she caught me lying or trying to pull the wool over her eyes. During her rant, I was freaking out. I wouldn't be allowed to do a goddamn thing anymore. Seriously my life would suck ass. I'd be like that writer in *Misery*. Kids locked up at the Institute would have more freedom than me.

I wouldn't speak to my mom at the dinner table. I was too pissed, especially since she kept giving me her smug, aren't-I-a-good-mother look as she ate her macaroni in tomato juice. She was proud of her latest move. It was written all over her face.

As soon as I finished eating, I shut myself in my room. I didn't help clear the table or do the dishes. I didn't even put my dirty bowl in the sink. The bitch could do it. I played a Blondie CD and lay down to think. I'd have to somehow work out a system to see Kevin and get more mesc. Kevin would dump me if we could never hook up.

Over the next weeks, I devised ways to get around my mom's rules. Me and Kevin started officially going out and arranged to see each other as often as we could at the bus station after school. There was like a twenty-minute gap between when my charter school bus would arrive and when the city bus I took home would leave. We'd basically use that time to make out, and Kevin would talk about music and also about the horror movies he'd just seen. He couldn't wait for my punishment to end so we could watch them together at his place. Ditto for me. And I was sick of just kissing. I wanted us to move on to more serious stuff.

As for my mesc, Eve would get it for me. I paid with the money my mom gave me for my school lunch pass each month. I'd secretly snort mesc at the condo before I'd leave for school in the morning or before my mom came home from work at five-thirty sharp. Some nights, I'd snort some after I'd hear my mom click off her bedside lamp. I hid it in a teddy bear on my bed. I'd pulled out a bit of his stuffing, just enough to slip a baggie inside. My mom would never think of looking there. You really couldn't tell my bear's stitching had come undone a bit. He just had a tiny hole in his lower back, and it wasn't visible unless you looked super close.

My dad would call from time to time to see what I was up to and check when I could go out to brunch with him and his girlfriend. My mom hadn't told him about finding the mesc and grounding me, so I'd make up excuses to avoid going. I had too much homework, I'd spend the long weekend with my head in a book, there was a party at our cabin, it was Eve's birthday, I was driving to Quebec City with my mom.

I knew if I toughed it out, my mom would eventually get fed up with watching me nonstop. I mean, she couldn't even spend the night at Paul's or eat out with a girlfriend. She must've been bored silly herself. She lowered her guard on Valentine's Day after Paul invited her for a romantic weekend in L'Anse St. Jean. She said no to the weekend, but she did eat out with him at a steak house. I stayed home, and she phoned like three times that evening to ask what I was doing and to check that I was all alone at the condo. After that, she started trusting me a lot more and gave me back my dad's check to deposit before it expired. I think it was a week after Valentine's. I'd better not let her down, she said when she handed me the check. I figured that meant I was no longer grounded.

THE NEXT FRIDAY, on my way home from school, I cashed my dad's check and then called Fred from a phone booth to see if I could drop by his place to buy some mesc. Good timing, he said, because he'd gone to Quebec City during spring break and just mixed a batch. I should stop by his apartment when his mom was at work. She did the four to midnight shift.

I took the bus since my mom wouldn't drive me to Fred's. He lived in Mill River, but at the bottom of the hill. My mom didn't like me going there because she claimed it was a sketchy neighborhood. She'd read in the paper that some girl had been raped in McLeod Park. I'd heard that story too and even knew who the girl was. Personally I thought she'd made the whole thing up. She was probably pissed at some guy who didn't want to hook up, so she went around telling everybody she got raped in the park to seem more interesting. She was a slut. Every guy in town had fingered that chick.

I accidentally got off the bus three stops before Fred's place. I was confused about where he lived because I'd only been there once, in the late fall. I'd have to walk another ten minutes. It really was a white-trash neighborhood, the lower part of Mill River. There was nothing but apartment buildings and snowbanks covered in soot. The air reeked because of the dog turds thawing out and all the garbage piled up behind the apartments. Some of the street lamps didn't work. I was scared of getting attacked. Maybe that girl from the paper hadn't made her story up after all.

On my way to Fred's, I saw some shifty-looking dude ahead of me on the sidewalk. His bomber jacket was undone and his snowmobile boots were unlaced. What was he doing just standing there? A nutcase, no doubt. The dude kept glancing my way. I tried acting normal, but as I passed him, I turned off my Discman so I could hear him if he tried attacking me from behind. In the end, though, the guy was just waiting for his dog, which was taking a piss behind a half-melted snowbank. Still, I'd worked myself up so much that I ran the rest of the way.

Fred answered the door. He looked cool with his newly shaved head, but he still had his godawful patchy blond whiskers. He made a strange face. He told me not to have a cow, but Melanie was there. She'd dropped by for some mesc too. I honestly didn't give a fuck. Actually, I couldn't wait to see her face when I'd walk in.

I wondered if the walls of Fred's bedroom were still painted black and covered in posters. He had some ultra rare posters, like a Led Zeppelin that used to belong to his dad when he was young. Fred claimed it was now worth three thousand dollars. I had my doubts because I'd seen the same poster for twenty bucks in the window of Planet Rock. It was likely a copy of the original, but still.

His dad had died of lung cancer when Fred was nine, which was why he always exaggerated when he spoke about his father. The way Fred talked, the sun had shone out of his dad's ass, even though everybody else said the guy had actually been a fucking jerk. Fred was always telling us how his father would bring him everywhere with him, even to the brewery. He said his dad had cut back on his hours at the plant to spend more time with his family. Before his cancer, he'd worked just twelve hours a week. The rest of the time, he'd veg out at the apartment and play Nintendo with Fred after school.

Fred had talked about the brewery and his dad the last time I'd come over. His mom had been there making dinner, and she called Fred's dad a son of a bitch as she was taking the shepherd's pie out of the oven. She was so riled up she grabbed the pie without oven mitts on. Though she must've burned herself, she didn't even seem in pain. Fred called her a lunatic, and we went to eat our dinner in his bedroom. He told me his mom didn't have any nerve endings in her fingertips because she'd destroyed them by carrying hot dishes for twenty years at the restaurant where she worked. He also explained why she hated his dad so much. She claimed he'd had no balls and gotten fired from every single job he'd ever had. His mom thought it was totally unfair she had to wait tables sixty hours a week because her husband hadn't managed to hold down a job.

I wondered how Fred had convinced his mom to let him paint his room black. My mom had vetoed my idea to paint mine black. Instead, I got stuck with a sucky forest green, which her decorator had insisted was a Zen color since it said so on the color chart she always lugged around in her purse. Anyways, Fred was damn lucky.

When Melanie saw me walk into the room, she pretended to search for something in her knapsack. I told her to relax. I wasn't mad about the Pascal situation. I'd moved on. Melanie seemed relieved and then got up from the bed to give me a kiss on the cheek. I wondered what was up with her because she'd lost like twenty pounds since Christmas. The change wasn't so obvious at school, but here with her tight Les Wampas T-shirt, I couldn't help noticing. With her new hair color, she looked almost hot. She'd used Paprika Flirt, and I bet she'd bought a Wonderbra too. How had she lost weight so fast? Seriously, she'd always been chubby. I couldn't figure it out. She was probably doing other drugs than just mesc. I'd heard speed melted the pounds right off, and I'd have to ask Eve if that was true because she'd know.

Fred took the mesc out of his knapsack. I gave him five twenties since I was placing a big order. I'd keep most for me but also give some to Eve. It'd be a gift of sorts to thank her for helping me out while I was cooped up at home.

I started making lines on the bedside table, which was black melamine and kind of grimy. It revolted me to think I'd be snorting Fred's filth. As my mom had told me umpteen times, melamine always showed every speck of dust, which was why she'd refused to have melamine furniture at the house we'd shared with my dad.

Fred's new mesc was fucking ace. He'd never used such insane PCP before. He'd cut it at .12, and it was still the bomb. It was green PCP. For some reason, the punks at D'Youville Square called it Chiclet PCP. People totally blitzed out on it. That PCP was so strong that the plastic bag that Fred had carried it in from Quebec City had started to melt by the time he'd crossed the wild-life reserve.

We put a Dead Kennedys CD on, and then Eve showed up. When she saw Melanie, she looked at me, stuck two fingers down her throat, and pretended to hurl. Melanie looked bummed out. I wasn't in the mood for our feud. I told Eve to hurry up and do some mesc so we could be stoned together. Fred made a few lines as wide as a freaking highway on the bedside table and let Eve go first. Then Melanie vacuumed hers up all in one go. I was surprised because she was already pretty wasted. Her and Fred must've started getting high right after school. Fred's pupils were so dilated you couldn't even see the green anymore, like he had two black holes instead of eyes. In fact, he said he'd better wait till the mesc he'd done earlier had worn off a bit. We listened to the Dead Kennedys all the way through and then some Big Bad Voodoo Daddy.

Weirdly enough, even though the PCP was the bomb, the mesc didn't burn our nostrils much. The dextrose mellowed it out. Usually, Fred mixed it with lactose, but there was a shortage in the region. He'd even trudged to the health-food store in Alma to hunt some down, but no go. All the dealers must've gotten their PCP at the same time.

Melanie wasn't talking much. She sat slumped on the bed, her back against the wall. She was probably perturbed because me and Eve were there. We'd hated her ever since that scene at the cabin, and she knew it.

Eve was telling us about a fight she'd had with the girls in her band over the Hole covers they were supposed to play at their next show. She said Courtney Love was a crazy bitch and had maybe even killed Kurt. Kevin thought the same thing. He'd told me it was like Yoko Ono with John Lennon, only worse.

At one point, Melanie started drooling—not a lot, but just enough that it grossed us out. Fred shook her a bit because she was too spaced out. I threw a stuffed animal at her, a big plush dolphin that Fred had won at the Beauce Carnival. Melanie didn't react right away. A couple seconds later, she tried speaking, but we couldn't understand a thing. She was babbling. We decided to leave her alone, and if worse came to worse, we'd drag her into the shower. But then she started throwing up. Eve freaked and yelled that Melanie was passing out. We'd never seen anybody OD before—except in *Pulp Fiction*. I admit we had no fucking idea what to do, especially since we had no adrenalin shot if she started bleeding from her nose like in the movie.

We waited a bit to see if Melanie would come to. Fred was jabbering about how we could bring her around by giving her some milk to drink. Eve was moaning that the room smelled like barf. We should open a window to give Melanie some air, she said. Despite everything, we thought it was kind of cool to see somebody overdose. I mean, Melanie looked a lot like Mia Wallace when she foams at the mouth and nearly bites it.

Melanie wasn't waking up. We waited a bit more, and eventually I gave her a few taps on the cheeks. Fred went to start the shower so we could put Melanie in it. She'd turned a weird color. Eve was cursing the damn window, which wouldn't budge. Melanie starting puking bile out the side of her mouth, and it dribbled down her T-shirt. She wasn't moving at all anymore, and I was scared she'd go into convulsions and die right then and there. We were freaking and thought of calling an ambulance, except there was no way we could because the neighbors would see it parked out front and ask Fred's mom what had happened.

We decided to go to the hospital in Melanie's car. It was really our only option. Eve knew how to drive even though she didn't have her license yet. The car was parked in the street behind Fred's building. While Eve went to get it, me and Fred grabbed Melanie by her ankles and under her arms. We checked in the hallway to see if any neighbors were around and then carried Melanie down from the third floor. The girl weighed like a ton, and in fact we almost dropped her twice on the stairs. To make matters even fucking worse, there was slush everywhere outside, and also slippery patches of ice. Eve was waiting in the Neon. When she saw us, she got out to open the back door. We threw Melanie on the back seat and then headed off to Chicoutimi Hospital. The whole way over, we kept imagining cop cars everywhere. "Always" was playing in the tape deck, so Melanie had been listening to Bon Jovi before coming to Fred's. What a major douche bag. We dumped her in front of the doors to the ER and then sped off.

Afterward, we left her car in the parking garage off Racine Street and then walked down to the bus station. We were starving. After that whole OD scene, it must've been like nine o'clock. Nothing much was open, so we traipsed into Mr. Hot Dog. I ordered a barbecue poutine, Eve got egg salad in a bun, and Fred wolfed down three hot dogs. I thought he was being a pig, given the circumstances.

We planned to tell Melanie the next day that we'd left her car in the parking garage. In the end, though, she spent three days in intensive care. Apparently they had to tube her and hook her up to a respirator because the doctors were afraid she'd inhale vomit into her lungs. A girl at school even told Eve that Melanie was freaking out so much when she woke up with a tube down her throat that they strapped her to her bed and knocked her out with gobs of tranquilizers that were even stronger than PCP. She no doubt had to speak to the hospital shrink too. It must've been a truly magical moment.

ME AND EVE had gone to the movies. It was $3.50 Wednesday, and we'd seen *Fargo*. Afterward, I called my mom from the bus station to say I'd sleep over at Eve's. My mom always wanted to know where I was and where I'd spend the night. I couldn't sleep over at a boy's house even if I was no longer grounded. My mom said I'd better be telling the truth and that she could always call Eve's mother to check if I was there. I told her to trust me. I promised to be at Eve's, and we wouldn't stay up late. Before hanging up, I also said I loved her. That way, she wouldn't phone. Eve headed home, and I took the Vanier bus to Kevin's place. He'd never invited me over, but I knew where he lived because we'd gone there to pick up his dad's tools from their shed when we were building the cabin.

They lived in a plain-looking house that had white vinyl siding and a small stoop with three steps. I went down the side of the house to tap on Kevin's bedroom window. His room was in the basement, and there was a Fender Stratocaster sticker on the window. I knocked softly to avoid waking his parents. Kevin drew up the venetian blind to check who was there. When he saw me, he looked real happy. He motioned for me to go around to the front door. He came to unlock it wearing AC/DC pajama bottoms. I had to laugh at what a music fanatic the guy was. He shushed me. His dad had just gone to bed and had to be at work at five in the morning.

In his room, we could talk without bothering his dad. In any case, his dad liked me. He'd said I was polite, and Kevin's mom worked at the bank with an aunt of mine. I was sure he wouldn't care that I was in the basement with his son. Kevin's dad was cool. A couple times, he'd given us beer and bought us smokes. He'd even come to the cabin on occasion to have a drink with us. He'd sit on the couch beside the potbelly stove and tell stories about when he used to steal copper with his cousin. Me and Eve thought Kevin's dad was like an ex-biker or something. Anyways, he was super nice to us.

The light in Kevin's room was turned down low, and *Night of the Living Dead* was in his VCR. Kevin looked so cute with his hair all messy. He had rings under his eyes, though, but maybe it was just a trick of the light. We sat on his comforter and talked about Melanie's overdose. Other kids on mesc had also ended up in the hospital that week. Kevin wasn't surprised: green PCP was real dicey. He smiled at me and gave me a quick peck on the cheek. He was different, Kevin. My mom would've said he was showing me respect, but I felt more like we were five years old and I was his little girlfriend. You would've never known he'd been suspended from school for a month for punching out a security guard in the cafeteria. He was lucky, though: the guy didn't press charges because Kevin's folks made Kevin go to his house to do yard work. Kevin said the guard was actually a pretty nice dude. Carl was his name, and he lived in St. Fulgence with his girlfriend and their three sheepdogs.

It was weird because I'd never seen Kevin's room. The walls were white, and he'd doodled all over them in pencil. He'd drawn faces of people I didn't know, and he'd also written stuff. He saw me examining the walls and asked if I wanted to draw anything. He was sure I was a good artist. I picked up a pencil lying on his desk and started sketching a sort of Mia Wallace with piercings. Kevin said the girl looked like me, and hey, why didn't I get my nose pierced? Excellent idea, I thought, but my dad would kill me.

I asked Kevin if he'd mind starting the film over from the beginning. I'd never seen the whole thing. He rewound it, and we sat on his bed to watch. It wasn't as scary as ghost stories or the *Friday the 13th* movies. I felt kind of sorry for the zombies for being the living dead and for being super hungry all the time. After the movie, we talked about George Romero and other stuff and listened to music turned down low till like four in the morning. Kevin lent me a clean sweatshirt, and we went to bed. We slept spooned together without anything happening. I remember that when I woke up in the morning, I wondered if maybe Kevin was gay. But then right away I realized his erection was poking me in the back. I turned over to see if he was still sleeping. Nope. He looked me in the eyes and kissed me. He said he loved me. I was in love as well, and I felt almost like crying, but I held back my tears. I said I guessed I loved him too.

I got up and checked myself out in the mirror in Kevin's room. I had bed-head but still rocked. I took some mesc out of my purse and asked if he wanted any. He said to put away the mesc and come back to bed. Getting trashed at eight-thirty in the morning was too hard-core for him. I didn't get what difference it made whether it was eight a.m. or midnight, but whatever.

I climbed back under the covers with Kevin, and we started kissing again. I pretended to be too hot and slipped off the sweatshirt he'd lent me. He got up to put on some music, and he still had a boner in his boxers. I can't say why, but I knew sex would work with him.

Kevin put on a Sonic Youth CD and came back to bed. He was breathing hard, and he asked if he could touch me. I laughed. Of course, he could. I was topless in his bed, so he could do anything he wanted to me. He didn't say a thing, but he took off my panties. I had no trouble at all putting Kevin's penis inside me. What a relief. I was normal after all. It felt really good—I mean, not earth-shattering, but still really good. It hurt a little at first, but after a while, I was fine. Kevin came in me, and he kind of freaked till I told him I was on the pill. It was about nine-thirty. I went to pee and then came back to his room, and he was looking for a music magazine, the one I'd seen atop the pile beside his bed. On the cover was the guitarist from Rage Against the Machine. I asked Kevin if we could do it again.

I TOLD THE CAB DRIVER to wait because I had no money to pay him. I went inside the Deauville to find my dad and ask for some cash. He didn't mind. He'd rather I call a cab than travel by bus. Public transit was dangerous. Anybody could take it. In fact, he'd seen some young hoodlums hop on the bus at the stop in front of the St. George Institute. I should avoid boys like that. They were bad apples.

In his last message on the answering machine, my dad said I had no choice: I had to come for brunch on Sunday. He had something important to tell me. For chrissake, I hated people scheduling things for me.

My dad had reserved a booth at the back of the restaurant. The table was right beside a big bronze statue of a bull. I always used to stare at it when I'd come here with my parents. We'd eat at the Deauville at least twice a week because my mom had said dinner shouldn't always be her responsibility. Sometimes we'd stay till one in the morning, even if I had school the next day. While my parents drank their Brazilian coffees, I'd draw the bull on the back of my placemat and talk to the waitresses. When I was really wiped, I'd fall asleep on the bench. My parents would wake me up when it was time to go. I remember that one time my dad fell asleep too. He was wasted. My mom and Clinton, the manager of the Deauville, had to put him on a swivel chair and roll him to our car. My dad didn't even wake up. My mom was pretty mad, and the next morning she told my dad she'd been ashamed of him.

For our brunch, I didn't get why my dad had chosen this booth. It was our family's table. I was pissed that his ditz with her gray roots was sitting there. It was like he wanted his girlfriend to take my mom's place. If I was him, I would've picked another restaurant. I mean, everybody knew my mom at the Deauville. I was sure the waitresses would wonder what my dad was doing with a woman who was like three times less pretty. It was insulting for my mom.

I ordered the brunch special knowing that as usual I wouldn't even eat half of it. My dad asked for two eggs and toast. He always had the same thing for breakfast whether he ate out or in. Two eggs sunny-side up, buttered toast and a thin slice of tomato. No potatoes or anything else.

One of the first times we went to Venezuela, back in the eighties, my dad strode into the hotel's kitchen to show the cooks how to make his breakfast. My mom called him a country bumpkin and kept telling him to eat fruit salad like everybody else. But for my dad, changing what he ate for breakfast was unthinkable. Besides, fruit gave him a stomach ache.

My dad's girlfriend ordered the same thing as me. She was obviously trying to be my friend. I barely looked at her during brunch, even when she'd speak to me. She took my side when my dad dissed my clothes. I looked ratty in my mom's old boots, my ripped jeans, and my faded black sweater, he said. If I wanted, he'd give me money to go shopping at Jacob. Even better, he'd open an account for me there. I could pick out anything I wanted and put it on his bill. He must've felt guilty because of the divorce. He always did that—handed me money or made some over-the-top gesture—when he was feeling bad. He probably guessed that I hated his girlfriend. He must've known she wasn't that good-looking. He still loved my mom. That was why he wanted to open an account for me at a clothing store at the mall. To get closer to my mom. He must've thought I'd tell her and that she'd think he was being a nice guy.

I told my dad I hadn't shopped at Jacob for like a hundred years. That place sold shitty clothes for prisses. He had to stop thinking I was Vanessa or Sarah and would win some damn academic award or become a lawyer like him. My dad glanced around to see if anybody had heard. I'd better lower my voice and watch my mouth, he said. Anyways, we weren't at the Deauville to talk about my friends or clothes. We had an important matter to discuss. My dad's girlfriend got up and said she was going to the ladies' room. I was sure my dad would announce that he was getting married or his girlfriend was pregnant or they were moving in together. Yet it made no freaking sense: she was way too old and way too ugly.

But child support was what my dad wanted to talk about. He explained that a psychologist friend told him it'd be better to give me the money directly. The guy had read an American study on the children of divorce. It said teens whose parents were separated should be treated like adults, so my dad had decided to give the child support to me rather than to my mom. I'd learn to manage a budget. Plus, I'd be sure my mom wouldn't blow all the money on herself.

I didn't really get why my dad would listen to his psychologist friend. He never took advice from anybody. But it was true I didn't know where the child support was going. I mean, my mom didn't buy many groceries and never bought my clothes, so obviously she was spending it on herself.

I told my dad that the new arrangement suited me just fine. I realized I could now buy all the clothes and mesc I wanted. The waitress came by to clear the table. Seeing my plate half full, she asked if I wanted a doggie bag, but I told her I hated eating reheated food. While she was taking our plates, my dad's girlfriend came back. I said I'd give her the number of my mom's hairstylist. She'd look way better as a blonde. My dad handed me twelve postdated checks. He went to pay, and I headed off to the coatroom with his girlfriend to get our jackets. When we left, I saw my dad had bought a new pickup, a Silverado. He had his guy at the dealership put stripes down the sides. He told me the design came straight from the States. A special order. I got in and buckled up, thinking a striped pickup truck was frigging cheesy. What was he, a construction worker?

When I got home, I put the checks on the kitchen counter. My mom was folding the laundry in the living room. I didn't know what to do with twelve postdated checks—could I deposit them all at once?—and I was counting on my mom to tell me. She asked what the checks were for. Well, her face totally fell when I explained to her the theory of my dad's psychologist friend. She started cursing and crying. Then she shut herself in her room, and I heard her talking about my dad to her friend Sandra. She said my dad and the shrink were fucking crazy. She was sure my dad had concocted the whole scheme to get back at her. He must've found out that she was seeing Paul and had landed a job at an accounting firm. When she came out of her room, her mascara had run and her lipstick had smeared. I kind of felt sorry for her. I wondered if she could make ends meet without the money from my dad. I was worried we wouldn't fly to Florida like she'd promised during the divorce. I told her I'd loan her some money if ever she needed it. She didn't answer me. Instead, she rushed out of the condo with only one arm through a coat sleeve and her scarf almost falling off. I watched her drive away. The back of the car skidded because she took the turn too fast as she zoomed toward the boulevard.

I decided to take a bath. I'd always liked long baths in the afternoon, but the tub in our condo was way smaller than the one in our old house. We'd had a whirlpool bath there. My dad had installed it one weekend when me and my mom were visiting Quebec City. He wanted to surprise her. She always dreamed of having a big bathtub like in *Scarface*, with gold faucets, statues, and a TV opposite. My dad had chosen a humongous tub made of fake marble, but he said the accessories would come later. My mom had tears in her eyes when she saw her new bathroom. I thought it was amazing too. I imagined we were mega-rich, maybe even millionaires, but I wasn't too sure. In any case, my dad must've made a shitload of cash. His freezer was likely overflowing with dirty money.

It was in our basement freezer that my dad would hide the lawyer fees he got paid under the table. He'd also store the files of his bigwig clients there. The freezer would get so full my mom would gripe that she had no room to freeze her meat. My dad claimed that if a house caught fire, the freezer would burn last, so it was the perfect place to hide money. Because of income tax, he couldn't put it anywhere else. He'd already gotten in trouble with the taxman when I was in first grade.

I remember I'd come home from school and seen three government vehicles and a cop car parked in our driveway. My mom was waiting outside with a policewoman. When I asked what was happening and if we were going to jail, my mom told me not to worry. Tax officials had come to seize my dad's files and search the premises because they suspected him of money laundering and tax evasion. My mom swore he'd done nothing wrong. I believed her then, but today I have to wonder. The investigators spent two days at our house. Me and my mom stayed at a hotel with the lady cop, who kept an eye on us. She'd even follow my mom to the bathroom because she was afraid my mom would destroy important papers. My parents weren't permitted to speak to each other while the investigators were searching the house. When I was allowed back home, I saw that the walls had been ripped open. The tax guys had found my dad's porn stash in the suspended ceiling of our basement. I later learned they'd actually watched all the videos right in our house. According to my parents, they wanted to see if my dad had filmed any documents or other stuff like that.

Anyways, on the day of the twelve checks, my mom called the condo in the evening while I was studying for a geography test and listening to music. She seemed to have chilled out. She said that although my dad was using me to get even with her, I could still keep the checks. But I needed to manage my money better than the thousand bucks I'd gotten for my birthday because I'd now pay out of my own pocket for my schoolbooks, clothes, bus pass, maxi pads, and all the other stuff she'd spent her time buying me. I joked that maybe I could give her a cut for groceries and the rent too. That wasn't a bad idea, she said. What a bitch and a half. Had she talked to my dad? I asked. She replied that she was at Paul's and would sleep over. She told me to eat properly and be on time for school in the morning.

My mom was spending more and more nights at Paul's and even talking about moving in with him. I didn't know if she fully trusted me again or was just testing me. She'd started crashing at his place for entire weekends and cutting me some slack like before. One time, when Paul came to pick her up, he told me they were giving me enough rope to hang myself. The bastard had seriously started thinking of himself as my father, and my mom didn't say a word. Paul was on my case because he'd invited my mom to Florida for the Easter holiday, but she'd said no because of me. They were stuck in town as a result. They couldn't go up to the mountains either because the snowmobile trails to the cottage had started to melt and in those conditions Ski-Doos weren't allowed in.

It was Wednesday evening, and my mom was sleeping at Paul's again. When she left the condo, I called Kevin to see if he wanted to spend the night. He showed up like ten minutes later, and I laughed and asked if he'd taken a teleporter. His dad had dropped him off. The guy was glad his son was going out with me. I was a nice kid, he said. It would be good for Kevin to hang around a girl with some class. He wouldn't be cooped up in the basement every night listening to music and covering the walls with his crazy doodles.

Kevin had brought two movies in his knapsack: *Faces of Death* and *Cannibal Holocaust*. I didn't know which to watch first, so we flipped a coin and *Faces of Death* won. Kevin told me that lots of countries had banned the movie, but Servideo had an uncensored pirated copy. Wow, it sounded totally brutal. I'd need to do some mesc before I watched it.

I still had a bit left over from that time at Fred's. If there was enough, Kevin would do some too. I made lines on the coffee table and then wiped it with Windex. If my mom saw smudges on her glass table, she'd lose her shit. I didn't feel like sitting through a lecture on how I'd mucked up her damn table and was never careful with her things. I threw the paper towel in the kitchen garbage and pushed it to the bottom so my mom wouldn't notice. She'd think it was fishy that I'd wiped the table since I wasn't exactly fanatical about housework.

Kevin put *Faces of Death* in the VCR, and we started watching. We were pretty wasted. I was seeing the screen in double, and the images were all blurry. I remember the movie was mega-disturbing. We saw Jews getting butchered in the Second World War and a truck smush this guy on a bike. The paramedics had to scrape his guts off the bottom of the truck, and his brains were splattered all over the road. I felt like barfing, so I turned to look at Kevin. He was so effing cute with his pompadour and his white T-shirt. He'd rolled the sleeves up and looked like a real rocker.

Right after, we watched *Cannibal Holocaust*, which was better than *Faces of Death*. There was a plot at least, plus some actors had apparently died during the film shoot. The scene where the cannibals impale a girl was seriously gruesome, so I hid my face against Kevin's neck. Did I want him to stop the video? he asked. I shook my head and then started kissing him. We had sex on the couch. The whole time, we could hear the characters in the movie dying one by one.

In the morning, we took the bus at seven-twenty and got to school on time. We'd stayed up the whole night listening to music and talking about *Cannibal Holocaust*. We wondered if it was true that some actors had died and if the director had actually killed animals for the movie. Kevin said the video store also had *Cannibal Ferox*, which the clerk claimed was even more hard-core than *Cannibal Holocaust*. The copy had been rented, but Kevin reserved it. We'd have it by the following Saturday.

I had civics first period that morning, and Kevin had English. I was still stoned because we'd done more mesc around six o'clock. The teacher's name was Mr. Guy, but everybody called him Mr. Gay behind his back. He did seem like a fag. He was tall and thin and a sort of Jesus freak. At one point, I was goofing around with the girl sitting beside me. What was I laughing about? Mr. Guy wanted to know. And why was I disturbing the whole class? Nowadays teenagers felt so entitled, he said, and just did whatever they pleased without a thought for anybody else. Then he spouted some dopey proverb: your freedom ends where mine begins. I snickered and told him to get down off his high horse. He got even madder, and everybody started laughing at him. He was annoying me big-time, so I called him Mr. Gay. Well, he wrenched me up by the arm and literally dragged me to the principal's office.

I had to wait on a chair beside the secretary's desk because the principal was already with a student. He hadn't shut the blind, and I could see the girl who was with him. I knew her. She was in ninth grade too and sold weed at the bus station. I'd spoken to her a couple times. Sophie was her name. She was crying in the office, and the principal seemed to be talking on the phone. He must've called her parents. I hoped he wouldn't be in the same frame of mind with me. I didn't want him blabbing to my mom or dad about what I'd said in civics. My dad would strangle me because he absolutely hated me being rude.

I sat waiting for like fifteen minutes. Then the secretary told me I could go into the office. The principal wanted to know why I'd been booted out of class. He sounded all disappointed in me, but I didn't give a hoot. He knew my parents were separated, yet that was no reason to turn into a hooligan and ruin my future. I'd changed since the start of the year, he said. I was hanging out with the wrong crowd and dressing sloppy and now I was talking back. My grades were slipping too, and he didn't know if I'd even pass ninth grade given my downward spiral. I rolled my eyes and told him to read my file. He opened the manila folder on his desk and made the face I knew he'd make when he saw my marks. I had the highest average in my grade, maybe even in the entire school: ninety-seven percent. It was right there on my last report card. I wasn't struggling at all. In fact, I might even win a goddamn Governor General's Medal if I kept at it. The principal made me promise to be nicer to Mr. Guy. He didn't call my parents. He didn't even give me detention.

When my mom got back from work around five-thirty, I told her there was a party at the cabin that night and I wanted permission to go. My mom refused because it was a school night. I said I had no homework and was going anyway. She threatened to tell my dad I was on the pill if I stepped out the door. He'd be sure to cancel his postdated checks if he knew. I yelled I didn't give a fuck and rushed off wearing my leather jacket and a pair of magic gloves. As I walked to the bus stop, I counted in my head how much money I had left in my bank account. Enough to buy a shitload of mesc and maybe tabs of acid too. Anyhow, I had time to deposit the next check before my mom made up her mind to talk to my dad. The next day was the first of the month. It'd take at least three days for her to drum up the courage to phone him.

I'd left home fast, so I wasn't really dressed for a party. I had on an old pair of flared jeans. I was really nervous about bumping into a girl from my crowd on the bus. My friends would all make fun of me if they knew I still had these pants in my closet.

I decided to go to Eve's so she'd lend me some clothes. We

could do our hair and makeup in her room, and maybe her mom would drive us to the trail. I just hoped she'd be home and not at Fred's.

I phoned her house from the bus station, and Eve picked up. She said to come over, but she wasn't dressed or showered yet. Had I had dinner? I lied that I had because I didn't feel like eating with her family, especially since her mom always served something weird. One time, she'd made this spicy Tunisian spaghetti, which was ultra revolting.

It took twenty minutes by bus to get to Eve's place. When we stopped in front of the St. George Institute, the type of guys my dad loathed got on. They traipsed to the back and started yelling some stupid shit. One boy was cute even though he still dressed like a skater, but Kevin was a thousand times better-looking.

The Institute dudes got off at the mall. I realized I hadn't been there in ages. The salesladies at Ardene and La Senza must've forgotten all about me, which meant I could go back to swipe some panties and earrings soon. I wondered if Eve would want to come. We'd never gone to Royal Plaza together. She obviously shopped, though, because she always had on something new.

I arrived at Eve's while her family was eating dinner. I was glad I'd lied because her mom had made some kind of gooey rice dish. She told me it was called risotto and came from Italy and that I absolutely had to try some even if I'd already eaten. I was like forced to sit down at the table with them. Eve's dad and twin brothers had almost finished their plates. I had no idea how to eat risotto. Eve said it was better with Parmesan sprinkled on top. She passed me some kind of space-age grater, which I didn't know how to use. As I fiddled with it, one of the twins told me just to turn the crank. I said duh, I knew what I was doing, I was no retard. In the end, I ate the whole damn plate. It was actually pretty tasty.

Me and Eve helped her mom clear the table and fill the dishwasher. Her dad came into the kitchen to ask if her mom needed anything from Canadian Tire because he was going there to change his drill. Meanwhile, the twins took off down the basement. No surprise there: they'd never hang around with Eve and me while I was over. They thought they were way cooler because they were older. It bugged me that I couldn't tell Christian and Nicolas apart. They were carbon copies of each other and equally cute. Plus, they were always together and would hit on the same type of girl. They'd even gone out with the Imbault twins for a couple months. Me and Eve thought that was pushing things too far, and we'd tease them that if they ever married those girls, their kids would be Siamese twins. Even though I said that, I was actually jealous. I wished I had twenty-year-old guys coming on to me.

Me and Eve went to her room. Her parents were loaded, so she had like a huge room with her own bathroom. Her dad worked in finance, and my dad would always call him a shark. My mom said my dad talked that way because he was green with envy.

Eve said she'd take a shower and asked if I wanted to join her. I didn't need a shower. I wondered if she really was a lesbian after all. I mean, why ask me to join her if she wasn't?

While Eve was in the bathroom, somebody knocked on her bedroom door. It was her mom with the cordless phone. Fred wanted to speak to Eve. I said I'd take the call since Eve was in the shower. Her mom handed me the phone, and I shut the door.

Fred asked when we'd be coming and if we had any mesc left from the batch he'd made before the Easter holiday. If we didn't, he'd bring more. I had hardly any left, and I'd need to buy tons before my dad blocked my checks. No prob. Fred would bring plenty for everybody.

After her shower, Eve dried her hair and rummaged through her drawers for clothes that would suit me. I chose a rad fringe sweater with a bald eagle and the American flag on it. It'd go great with tight black jeans and my boots. On my eyes, I drew a line with black Revlon eyeliner and stuck on some sequins for extra sparkle. Then I used a flat iron to straighten my hair for a Mia Wallace look. I totally killed. Kevin would freak when he saw me.

Eve left her hair loose. It was brown and really long, and just after she washed it, she'd look like the curly-haired model from the Alberto VO5 commercial. I was jealous of her hair even though she was always telling me she wanted straight hair like mine.

I told Eve to put on her black leather pants since they made her look super slim and gave her a nice butt. With her leopard-skin bustier, she'd really rock. She asked me to do her eyes because she was clueless with makeup. She'd always mess up her eyeliner and end up with a hideous dotted line above her eyelids. It'd be a major drag if the other girls pointed it out.

Around eight o'clock, Eve's dad dropped us off at the entrance to the trail. He told us to be careful and to take it easy on the boys. We laughed, promised not to break too many hearts, and then got out of the car.

It was really dark on the side of the road and pitch-black on the trail. The spruce trees blocked the moon. We felt like idiots for not asking one of the guys to come meet us with a flashlight.

We walked pretty slow because the trail was muddy—even though there were still patches of snow in the woods—and also because we could barely see a thing. I was scared I'd stumble over a rock or a tree stump. I'd left my winter boots back at the condo, so I was also afraid of getting my snakeskin boots dirty. When we heard some branches snap in the woods, Eve yelped and stopped dead in her tracks. I was forced to stop too. I faked a panicky voice and said the ghost of the murdered partridge was after us. That wasn't funny, she said, all mad. I told her she was such a wuss. After we listened awhile to the night around us, she started along the trail again. As we were walking, I said it'd be cool to see those UFO lights my mom's boyfriend had seen. Eve told me to shut up already. She said she couldn't understand why we hadn't reached the stream yet, that it didn't make any sense. I could hear in her voice that she was about to freak. She said maybe we'd gotten lost. As if, I said. We continued on our way and, wouldn't you know, we came to the stream like two minutes later.

When we arrived at the cabin, the guys were doing hot knives with a blowtorch on the porch. They'd started smoking up outside now that the temperature was above zero because otherwise it'd really reek inside. Kevin was doing hits with Simon, Fred and Pascal. There were also these two spiky-haired punks sitting on the porch, but I didn't know them. They must've come up from Quebec City to be decked out the way they were. Punks from Chicoutimi didn't wear their hair like that, and I'd never seen punks who let their suspenders hang down their pants and who tied their eighteen-holes with white laces. Fred was talking to one of them, probably his PCP connection. Melanie wasn't around—thankfully. Ever since she'd come out of the hospital, she thought she was our best friend because we'd saved her life. OD'ing hadn't made her less of a loser. Lately her parents were keeping her on a short leash, and she was likely confined to her room twenty-four hours a day. Poor little shit.

I didn't toke up. Pot made me nauseous. The last time I'd smoked it, I'd touched the stretchy flap of skin underneath my tongue and it'd seriously weirded me out. Kevin came over to say he had to talk to me. I didn't understand why he had his knapsack over his shoulder. He asked me to go with him to the boulder behind the cabin. I wanted to head inside because my feet were cold in my thin boots, but he insisted. It had to be important since he wasn't the type to kid around. I followed him out back.

I was paranoid he was breaking up with me. He laid his knapsack in his lap and unzipped it. He took out five tapes and told me to put them in my purse. Nobody could see them. I was dead wrong about him dumping me. The tapes were a gift. Kevin had copied my favorite songs and his, and on the last tape he'd recorded groups I didn't know but would flip out over. He made me promise not to lend the tapes to anybody. The situation was pretty intense, so I was like totally bowled over. Obviously Kevin was the love of my life and he'd take me on a trip to Berlin one day. I remember I kissed him a long time on that big rock, and then it started to drizzle, so we went inside.

In the cabin, Eve and Fred were doing mesc on the card table. There was a pile of two-fours in a corner—four cases—and I thought what the fuck since we never drank much beer. Kevin had brought them. I wondered where he'd gotten the money. His dad must've paid him for helping out on a job. I didn't get why Kevin had sprung for beer for everybody since we had our mesc and acid and the Quebec City punks had also brought lots of other excellent stuff I'd never tried before. We didn't need beer too, but Kevin told me he felt like throwing the party of the century.

Everybody was all fired up that night. Eve had dropped acid and was jabbering away, telling me like four stories at once that I couldn't follow. I hadn't done acid because I didn't feel like staying awake all night. Besides, I was already flying high. The punks kept trying to take control of Kevin's boom box, and I laughed as I watched them. They'd better forget it because Kevin didn't give a shit what they wanted to hear. To piss them off even more, he put on a Chuck Berry song. Meanwhile, Eve was rattling on about how her mom loved her brothers more than her. So bogus. Man, that girl could invent problems for herself. I told her to stop her babbling and come dance with me.

At one point, somebody started banging on the front door. I didn't know what time it was, but it had to be late because hardly anybody was still around. We wondered if we were hallucinating. I remember I was really wasted and just stayed slumped on the couch. Eve got up, but before she could take two steps, the door swung open and in came my dad. He looked like he wanted to rip my head off. Then I saw my mom standing in the doorway and looking all panicky. I was freaking. There were empty baggies everywhere and leftover mesc on the table. My dad ordered me to put on my coat. He grabbed me by the arm. We were going home that minute. I was looking for Kevin but couldn't see him anywhere. Just his boots were there, next to the door. My dad told me to fall in line and march. There'd be no drug addict in this family. If he had to, he'd lock me in the basement till I turned eighteen. We headed outside. I assumed Kevin had gone home already, but why hadn't he worn his boots? Maybe he was so stoned he'd mixed them up with another guy's boots.

We practically flew down the fucking trail. My mom and dad were yapping about rehab and the St. George Institute the whole way. When we got to the pickup, my dad ordered me into the back seat. We took off toward the condo. I wasn't coming down at all from my high, and the lights on St. Genevieve Boulevard were hurting my eyes. For chrissake, I didn't need this. Plus, the two of them had teamed up. I wondered what would happen next. I knew I was in deep, deep shit.

At the condo, they asked if I was feeling all right. I was A-okay, man, just feeling a little faint. But I didn't say that. I didn't want them rushing me to the hospital to have doctors ram a frigging tube down my throat and pump out my stomach again. I couldn't help it—I started giggling. This was no laughing matter, my mom said, her bottom lip quivering. Me and my dad sat down at the kitchen table, and he told me he knew I was doing drugs. My mom brought us glasses of water and then sat next to my dad. There was a brochure on drug abuse lying on the table.

My dad launched into this story about an old buddy of his who'd smoked pot once and gone nuts. The guy had thrown a party in the basement of the house he'd shared with his mother. At one point, he went upstairs and came back down with a bowl of chips. The next morning, they found his mother dead on the kitchen floor. He'd stabbed her. My dad's friend must've heard voices or had some kind of psychotic episode. My dad never found out for sure, but the guy was sent to jail for twenty-five years. My dad never touched drugs again after that. He was convinced that weed had driven his friend to kill his mother.

My dad had always been a good liar, and I was sure he'd made up that story to scare me. No dude would kill his mom after smoking one joint. I didn't tell my dad I didn't buy his story, though. That would've only made things worse. Instead, I said I didn't smoke pot. My dad got all steamed and ordered me to tell him what I was on then. I didn't answer. Anyhow, my mom had started sobbing so loud we could barely hear each other. I asked my dad if I could go to bed. It was late, I was exhausted, and there was school in the morning. I'd take the day off, he said. We'd be meeting with a counselor at the Institute. I'd crossed a line this time, but not to worry because they wouldn't lock me up, not right away. They just wanted me to talk to a professional about my drug problem. Oh, for fuck's sake. I told myself I could tell those social workers anything. I knew exactly what to say so they'd leave me alone: I'd talk about the divorce.

It was eleven when I woke up the next morning. I felt like shit and probably looked like hell. My mom came into my room without knocking. She was crying, and her face looked sort of discombobulated. I told her to stop freaking out. I wasn't like a total drug fiend.

My mom had the cordless phone in her hand. She passed it to me and said to call Kevin's dad. He'd phoned earlier while I was sleeping and wanted me to call him as soon as I woke up. He was probably looking for his son. I knew Kevin had left our cabin without his boots.

Kevin's mom answered, but she was weeping on the line and I couldn't understand a thing she said. She must've been worried sick. I told her not to panic, that Kevin had likely just crashed at a friend's place and hadn't woken up in time for school.

The line went quiet, and then Kevin's dad came on. He spoke my name and then told me that something had happened to Kevin. He'd hanged himself in the night. His mom was the one who'd found him. I said no, no, that was impossible. He said he had to get off the phone.

I sat there in a complete and utter daze. I kept thinking of something I'd once read in a trashy tabloid of my dad's. It said that when you hanged yourself, you'd see little spots of yellow light before your eyes.

I remember that after I got off the phone, my mom came back into my room. She sat on my bed, and I cried for a long time pressed up against her terry velour bathrobe. My mom stroked my hair, and for once she didn't speak. There was really nothing to say.

Eventually I got a grip on myself. My mom brought me a glass of water and then phoned my school to say I'd be away at least a week. The secretary didn't ask any questions, so Kevin's folks must've already notified the school. My mom told me to call her if I didn't feel well or needed anything. Then she closed my bedroom door gently behind her.

I don't know why, but that day I was convinced I'd feel a bit better if I didn't spend the whole day in my nightie. I opened a dresser drawer to pick out a T-shirt. Everything was in a total jumble, so I decided to straighten the drawer out. I emptied the whole thing on my bed and began reorganizing my clothes. My mom had taught me how to fold T-shirts properly by bringing the sleeves into the middle and then folding the top toward the bottom. It'd looked simple when she'd shown me, but at that moment I found it super hard and couldn't do it right. I rummaged through the pile and decided it'd be easier to start with my tank tops. I came across my old sweatshirt from Three Salmon Summer Camp. It'd probably still fit, I thought. I had some trouble getting it over my head, but it wasn't too, too small. I went to my closet to get an old pair of jeans. The floor of my closet was a hodgepodge of shoes and old school assignments and hangers that had fallen down. I took everything out and started sorting through my shoes. Lots of them I hadn't worn in ages. I threw my Kickers and Stan Smiths into a corner of my room. I'd go toss them in the dumpster later.

My mom knocked on my door and came in before I could answer. She'd heard my racket all the way in the kitchen even with the dishwasher running, and she was worried. And how come my clothes and shoes were strewn all over the room? I didn't say anything about my clothes. I said no way would Kevin have committed suicide. It was totally impossible. It didn't make any sense whatsoever, and I knew his parents hadn't told me the whole story.

My mom came over to my bed and plunked herself down. She pushed my clothes aside so I could sit next to her. No, his parents hadn't told me everything, she said, but I couldn't blame them. They were in shock. I should try to put myself in their shoes. Her comment was a bit mean, I thought. Earlier, while I was still sleeping, Kevin's dad had explained to her what had happened. She patted my arm and said I was old enough to know. She didn't look too sure, though, but she started telling me nonetheless.

Kevin had come home from the cabin around midnight and decided to make himself some french fries. Apparently he'd often do that when he got home late. He put the fries in the oven and headed down to the basement. The smoke detector eventually started blaring and woke Kevin's mom. The whole house smelled of smoke because the fries had burned to a crisp in the oven. She went downstairs to see if Kevin had fallen asleep and forgotten his fries. When she got to his room, she just saw a pair of boots and his wool sweater. She looked around the basement awhile and then thought of checking the garage just in case. That was where she found him. He'd stepped off a stool. There were lots of tools knocked down and lying on the floor around him. Kevin must've tried to pull himself up or find a foothold somewhere along the wall.

WE ALL WENT to the funeral home to see Kevin. Even Melanie came. She must've gotten special permission from her folks, who probably thought seeing a dead body would serve as a lesson. Of course, all our parents thought the same thing. Drugs had killed Kevin. He'd still be alive if it wasn't for drugs. Mescaline had made him go psycho. PCP was for horses, after all, so it was super strong. It went straight to your brain and could even gouge out holes in it. A cop who'd once come to our school to warn us about drugs said so. When I heard that, I understood why I had one nostril thinner than the other. It was the mesc. It made perfect sense because if PCP could melt plastic, it could sure as hell melt your nostrils, eat holes in your brain, and make you crazy enough to hang yourself.

Just before we went in to see Kevin, we gathered in Rosaire Gauthier Park. It was me, Fred, Eve, Pascal and Melanie. Just the five of us, nobody else. Fred had brought his boom box, some vinegar chips and some Molson XXX beer. We put on the latest CD by Les Wampas. It'd just come out, and Kevin had been playing it nonstop. As we listened to *Too Precious*, we snorted some mesc. Fred still had his connection for green PCP, and he only mixed with the green stuff now. Eve made some lines for Kevin like he was there with us. After we all snorted our own lines, we blew Kevin's mesc into the wind. Then we observed five minutes of silence. There was no snow left on the ground, and it was starting to get real warm out. Crows were circling us with their big wings and their creepy cawing. They wanted our leftover chips. I'd told the others a hundred times not to feed the crows, but they thought the birds were cute and would give them anything to eat. I was sure those fucking crows would end up pecking somebody's eyes out.

Kevin was at Gravel & Sons Funeral Home opposite the park. I was stoned and didn't want to see his parents. I was scared I'd start bawling. His dad was sitting on the steps at the entrance and smoking a cigarette. Peeking out of his blazer pocket was a little bookmark with Kevin's face on it. When his dad spotted me coming across the parking lot, he got up, walked over, and gave me a big hug. He started crying, and I felt so awkward. I wanted him to let me go. I wanted him to stop his weeping and just leave me alone, but instead he took my hand and led me inside to see Kevin.

I flinched when we walked into the room reserved for Kevin. He was lying in a white casket with angels engraved on the sides. All around him were baskets of flowers, and you could smell those lilies even out in the lobby. I thought the casket might be closed because he'd hanged himself, but the lid was up and there were no marks on his neck. Before I left for the funeral home, my mom assured me Kevin would look like he was sleeping. Well, that was total bullshit. He looked like he'd been stuffed by a taxidermist. Plus, he was wearing a suit, and his face was covered in thick makeup. To hide the rope marks on his neck, maybe the undertakers had applied some five-hundred-dollar foundation like my mom's makeup artists had used.

Kevin's dad wouldn't let go of my hand. I looked for Eve but couldn't spot her with Pascal and the others. She was likely in the restroom snorting more mesc. I wished I was with her. But then again, Kevin would've thought it was pretty shitty of me to get blitzed in front of his dad.

Kevin's mom appeared at the head of the casket. Her eyes were red, but she wasn't crying. Her doctor must've given her some sedatives. She was staring at Kevin and stroking his hair. She had such a handsome son, she muttered. Kevin would've freaked out because she was messing up his pompadour. She said she'd decided to put him in the nice suit she'd bought him for his cousin's wedding the summer before. Kevin would've been pissed. He hated suits. I was sure he would've wanted to wear his tight black jeans and his Stooges T-shirt. He looked like a homo decked out in that suit. Still, I told his mom he really did look handsome.

The funeral home was packed. The room Kevin was put in was too small to fit the whole town, so the funeral director had also opened the adjoining room. By midafternoon, though, the place was so full that people were waiting in line outside to get in.

The entire school came, even the principal and the teachers. Mr. Guy showed up too. I stayed next to Kevin with his mom and dad. People came to offer us their condolences, and when they'd get to me, they'd hug me and say some pretty intense stuff I didn't really want to hear. I prayed it'd end soon. I would've preferred to be alone with Kevin, and I was sure he would've felt the same way.

At one point, I spotted my dad in the lobby leaning against the doorway to the columbarium. I was surprised he turned up. He hated funeral homes and people getting all weepy. My mom hadn't come. She was terrified of dead bodies. My dad stood in that doorway for like fifteen minutes. Eve's mom joined him, and as they talked, they kept glancing my way. My dad was wearing one of his lawyer suits and had just had a haircut.

I knew my grandma's urn was in the columbarium, but he didn't look like he'd go in. He still hated his mother and had called her a psychopath my whole life. They didn't even make up when she got bladder cancer. My dad told me that the last time he'd seen her at the hospital, she'd chewed him out for being late and not shaving. I knew he'd gone to patch things up with her, but she'd been so bitchy that he just couldn't. Before fleeing the hospital, he'd told her she'd never in her life see his face again.

I was scared my dad would blab to Eve's mother about the mesc. She was way less gullible than my mom. Eve wouldn't get a second chance: she'd be shipped right off to boarding school in Dolbeau. Her mom started crying. I knew my dad didn't know what to do with himself. She took a Kleenex from her purse and dabbed at her eyes. My dad gave her three little taps on the shoulder and then went to stand in line for the condolences.

Eve, Fred, Melanie and Pascal were sitting on chairs at the back of the room and trying to console each other. I would've given anything for this to be a bad dream and for us to wake up in Rosaire Gauthier Park with Kevin. Spring this year would come earlier than usual, and we'd bet on the date when all the ice on Lac St. Jean would be melted. I'd go to the hole with Kevin, and he'd ask me to light the campfire. Maybe my mom would even invite him to spend a weekend at the cottage. He'd help Paul fix the floating dock and drag the pontoon boat back into the water. My dad would think Kevin was a fine young man. Kevin would come to my birthday dinner and give me some rad gift, and he'd still be alive.

People filed past us offering their sympathies. They all said more or less the same thing: time healed all wounds, they'd be there for us if we needed them, it made no sense for a boy to die so young. I didn't know how to reply. I felt out of place there with his parents, but Kevin's dad wouldn't let me leave. He was gripping my hand so tight it was going numb.

When it was my dad's turn, he told me he was so, so sorry. I started bawling. I couldn't help it. I even had trouble breathing and thought I might throw up. My dad held me in his arms and asked under his breath if I wanted to step outside for some air. Kevin's mom also started bawling. Eve too. I think everybody in the whole damn room was crying by that point, but I was sobbing so loud that the funeral director came over to take me to a small private room. My dad said if I needed him, he'd be in the lobby. The director led me to a sort of lounge and then drew a big gray velvet curtain closed. There was a floral couch, a coffee table and a box of Kleenex. I sat on the couch and tried to calm down. Eve came in, and we cried in each other's arms till my dad and her mom arrived to get us. The funeral home would be closing in twenty minutes.

I didn't want to leave right then. I wanted to go see Kevin and speak to him one last time. I'd seen his pinkie finger move,

I was sure. Maybe he wasn't really, truly dead. The doctors might've made a mistake. I'd seen something similar once on the documentary channel. A lady in the States was declared dead by her doctors, and she later woke up in a drawer at the morgue. A janitor at the hospital rescued her after hearing her banging with all her might to get out. Kevin would go crazy if he woke up locked in a drawer. Then he'd die for real.

My dad held me by the shoulders and tried to convince me we should go. He was heartless, I yelled. He should just leave me the hell alone. He was never there when I needed him anyway. He should go back to his ditz, and I'd walk home by myself. My dad said we'd come back to see my boyfriend. We headed out of the lounge, and I saw that almost nobody was left in the funeral home. My dad put his arm around my shoulders and escorted me outside.

In the parking lot, everybody was talking and smoking in little groups. We'd just started heading toward my dad's pickup when the funeral director came rushing out with my purse. I'd left it on the couch. He went back inside, and when I saw him lock the door to the building, I couldn't deal and started sobbing hysterically again. Everybody turned to look. My dad said not to concern myself with the others. Kevin's mom was watching me. She looked like she wanted to say something, but she kept quiet as I walked past. My dad helped me into the pickup and buckled my seatbelt. He went around the truck, got in and started the engine. Did I want to get a bite to eat somewhere before he dropped me off? I wasn't hungry, I said.

My mom was waiting in the lobby of our building. My dad told her I needed some rest. She thanked him for going to the funeral home, and then me and my mom headed inside our condo. I was still crying a bit, and I told her that maybe Kevin wasn't really dead. She asked if I'd taken anything, and I said no. She didn't look like she believed me. I lay down on the couch, and she went into her room. I heard her call the poison control center to find out if she could give me a sleeping pill even if I'd done drugs. No, she didn't know what I'd taken, she said on the phone. Maybe PCP, but she wasn't sure. She hung up and came back with a small plastic vial. They'd said it'd be all right, she whispered, handing me a green pill. I was scared to take it. What if I OD'd or if the pill fried all my brain cells?

I laid my head in my mom's lap, and we watched a movie on TV. I don't remember what it was, though, because the sleeping pill had kicked in. My mom smelled nice, and her bathrobe was as soft as a kitten. I let her stroke my hair, and I replayed the night at our cabin in my head. I couldn't believe we hadn't noticed anything wrong. I kept thinking that while I'd been getting totally wasted with Eve, Kevin had been trying to save himself. I imagined him panicking when he'd realized he couldn't pull himself up and would die on the end of that rope. But maybe he hadn't realized it and had blacked out without suffering too much. God, I hoped so. I wondered if he'd thought about me at all. My head still in my mom's lap, I drifted off into a dreamless sleep.

THE HORROR MOVIE section was just beside the porn. While I was looking for *Cannibal Ferox,* a guy pushed through the swinging doors that separated the XXX videos from the regular movies. It had to be Big Steve. Kevin had told me about him. People in town said he wasn't all there, and they called him Fathead. He hadn't gotten enough oxygen at birth, so he was retarded. Big Steve was six foot four and had long tangled blond hair. He looked like a Viking. All the clerks at Servideo knew him because he came to rent porn almost every day. Kevin had told me that a clerk had once caught Big Steve jacking off. He'd jizzed all over a Jenna Jameson video. The clerk bawled him out and said if he ever caught Big Steve beating off again, he'd ban him from the store for life. The guy didn't call the police or anything. Big Steve had the maturity of a three-year-old, so people felt sorry for him and left him alone as long as he stayed out of trouble.

Big Steve came out of the porn section after about two minutes with three videos. He looked my way and gave me a big stupid smile. He told me the weatherman was expecting a high of twenty-two Celsius. I didn't know what to say. I'd never spoken to a real retard before. I continued looking for my film, and Big Steve left the store and no doubt went home to play with himself.

I hadn't been to Servideo since the *Red October* incident with my dad, and I couldn't figure out how they were now grouping their videos together. I mean, the *Friday the 13th*s were mixed with the *Halloween*s. They were missing some *Freddy*s, and I couldn't see a single *Chucky* anywhere. Yet there were a lot of videos with scary covers that I'd never seen before. I thought I'd rent *Eraserhead* with Eve another time. I couldn't find *Cannibal Ferox* or *Cannibal Holocaust*, so I got fed up and went to ask.

The clerk—a tall skinny dude wearing a Megadeth T-shirt and leather bracelets—was alone at the till sorting through the returns. I told him I couldn't find *Cannibal Ferox*. No duh, he said. He didn't shelve it with the other horror movies because the store had had some complaints. He kept it behind the counter, but he couldn't rent it to me because somebody had reserved it. I said I knew who and that Kevin had told me I could come pick it up. The guy threw me a weird look. He hesitated for like ten seconds and then bent down to find the video. When he stood back up, he asked if I realized how hard-core the movie was. I said yeah and that I'd seen *Cannibal Holocaust*. The dude seemed to figure out I was no wuss and then put the video in a white plastic bag with SERVIDEO written across it in blue. He bent down again to rummage under the counter. He took out three more videos and added them to the bag without showing me what they were. He held out the bag. He said for me there was no charge and that he'd lent me a couple more movies I'd like. I thanked him and then split with the videos. It really was hot out, and it wasn't even noon.

147

I was lying in bed when the phone rang. I didn't feel like getting up even though it was already nine o'clock. I'd woken up a bit earlier and was thinking about school. I hadn't gone in like a month. Eve had said everybody was asking about me and that some people were saying I was using Kevin's death as a free pass to stay home and veg out. My mom had spoken to the principal. They'd agreed I'd finish the school year at home and show up only for exams. I was glad because I wasn't in the mood to see people and hear their questions. Already whenever I'd bump into kids I knew, they'd ask why Kevin had killed himself. Had there been signs? Had he left a suicide note?

It was my dad on the phone. He invited me to go for breakfast at Mount Royal Café. We needed to talk. I said okay. In any case, it wasn't like I had a choice with my dad. Plus, I was hungry and hadn't had bacon in a while. I usually skipped breakfast because I'd snort mesc in the morning, but I had none left. When I got out of bed, I poked around my bookshelves in case I'd forgotten a baggie somewhere. I'd occasionally hide some mesc in *Christiane F.* or *The Valley of Horses*. I didn't find any, though.

At the restaurant, I ordered the trucker's special. I hadn't seen my dad since the funeral home, and he was looking good. I ate everything but the baked beans since they were in a gross tomato sauce. I asked where Joanne was. My dad said she'd booked a spa getaway with a girlfriend. It was some sort of shaman thing in La Malbaie. She'd sleep in a log cabin in the woods for a week and see her totem. My dad didn't really know much about it. All he knew was it'd cost an arm and a leg.

He wanted to know if I'd like to spend some quality time with him. I almost burst out laughing. He sounded like a brochure. The two of us could go fishing together on Cement Shoes Lake one weekend. He was free in July. I must've made a weird face because my dad added that maybe I was using drugs because him and me never spent time together. Man, he thought he had all the answers. I said I wasn't even on drugs anymore. Given what had happened to Kevin, I was terrified of drugs now. He looked satisfied. He made me swear I'd never touch that crap again. Then he called over the waitress, who came by and asked if we needed anything else. His eggs were overdone on the bottom, he said, but he didn't have time for the cook to make him another order. We were in a hurry, and he wanted the bill. He left cash on the table but no tip, and then we took off. I'd thought our breakfast would last longer. I read in my room for the rest of the afternoon.

That evening, my mom had organized a dinner at the condo with Paul. I'd invited Eve because we were having Chinese fondue. On the table were strips of beef and cubes of chicken, as well as tiger prawns and sea scallops, which Paul had obviously bought since my mom wasn't nuts about seafood. Me and Eve stuffed ourselves with the prawns. I even had a second baked potato. Eve said she was totally stoked about her summer vacation because she was going to Cape Cod with her folks. Me, my mom and Paul didn't say much except that the hot sauce was a bit too spicy and it'd be fun to go to the waterslides in August.

After dessert, I asked my mom if I could sleep over at Eve's. We'd watch movies but wouldn't go to bed too late. Her dad had already given permission and could pick us up around eight. My mom nodded yes, but before I left, she had something to tell me. At the end of the summer, we'd be moving in with Paul. He had a big beautiful house in Chicoutimi North near St. Anne's Cross. I'd have a large room to myself. If I wanted, I could even paint one wall black—but only one. Paul said we'd all get along great, but he ran a tighter ship than my mom. I'd have to report in regularly and come home before midnight. I'd need to work on my manners too and help with the housework. As for drugs, if ever he found any or even suspected I was using again, I'd be sent off to the Institute pronto. I promised I'd never touch that stuff again and then asked if we could be excused and wait for Eve's father in my room. My mom said okay and that her and Paul would clear the table.

In my room, Eve said she had a present for me. She took two tabs of acid out of her purse. We dropped the acid and then called her dad to come get us. We didn't want the acid kicking in while we were in the condo, but her dad couldn't come right away because he was watching the end of some thriller with her mom. I told Eve we could just listen to music while we waited. I put on one of Kevin's mixtapes, and the first song was "Space Oddity," which got me a bit down. Eve asked if I was thinking of Kevin. Yeah, I was. She couldn't understand either what had come over him. Everybody had adored the guy. We didn't speak for the rest of the song. The tape was almost entirely Bowie, but we didn't mind. I started feeling high. Eve was moving all twitchy, and her pupils were so dilated she looked like an owl. We sat down on the floor, and I said her acid was fan-fucking-tabulous. Eve laughed at that expression, so I started making up others like "stu-fucking-pendous" and "mind-fucking-boggling." Eve said it'd be cool if chips came in flower flavors like tulip and daisy. We must've kidded around like that for a good hour before my mom came into my room. Eve's dad was at the front door waiting for us. My mom saw right away we'd taken something. She told Eve to go home without me and ordered me to bed. We'd talk in the morning about what I'd done, but just then she was too mad to discuss it. Eve hurried off.

I fell asleep at like six in the morning on account of the acid and woke up around eleven. When I came out of my bedroom to go to the bathroom, my mom and her boyfriend were sitting at the kitchen table with the same cop who'd come to my school early in the year to talk about drugs. Dan Bédard was his name. My mom said her and Paul would go for a walk and that the officer had some things to discuss with me. I sighed and waited for the dude to launch into his speech.

Dan took some photos out of his briefcase. One of them showed Fred selling drugs at the bus station. Another showed me buying mesc. Fuck. There was even a photo of Eve, Pascal and me getting high behind Mr. Hot Dog. And a photo of Kevin in front of Galaxy Arcade. That one really hit a nerve. Kevin looked so cute with his black beanie, his big eyes, and his leather jacket. Dan asked if I understood why he was there. I didn't say a word. My goose was cooked, man. St. George Institute, here I come. Dan said me and my friends were busted and that he'd been watching us since late fall and knew everything we'd been up to. He asked why I was hanging out with those losers and wrecking my life. People on hard drugs always ended up in the gutter. I was a pretty young woman and smart, and I had good parents. It didn't make sense to him. But if I wanted, I could turn my life around and he'd help me. There were programs for teens struggling with drug problems. The dude was in full lecture mode.

I looked Dan right in the eye and said he'd turned out all right despite being the biggest acid dealer in Chicoutimi in the seventies. I knew because Kevin's dad had told us. The secret had slipped out after he'd knocked back a couple beers, and he'd made us swear never to mention it to anybody. That rumor was a fat lie, Dan insisted. But the guy was all flustered, I could tell, because he immediately packed up his photos and got up to go. I was positive he'd tell my mom that me and him had an understanding. He'd say he'd scared me straight and that I'd keep my nose clean from now on.

My mom and Paul came back not long after Dan left. Paul looked seriously peeved and wouldn't talk to me the rest of the day. In the evening, after he went home, my mom came to my room. She'd lost all trust in me. I'd be grounded the whole summer, she said. I was also forbidden to see Eve, who she called a bad influence. My dad would take me on a fishing trip for my birthday, but that would be my only time away. The rest of the summer, we'd do things as a family with her boyfriend. He'd just bought a big boat for his cottage, and I'd learn to water-ski.

I'd also meet with a social worker who specialized in drug abuse. If I didn't cooperate, she really would send me to the Institute. The meetings with the social worker wouldn't start till late August because the lady wasn't available right away. I was safe for the time being, but oh man, would the summer be long.

My dad came to get me in his pickup on my birthday. He parked out front and beeped three times fast. He'd told me the night before that he'd wait for me in his truck. Him and my mom got along way better if they never crossed paths, and he saw no reason to change that. He knew my mom would be home: like him, she was on vacation till the first week of August. I'd packed my bag after lunch. I had to be ready because my dad hated waiting for me when we went up into the woods. My mom wished me happy birthday again and told me to bring her back a few big trout. One of my dad's buddies had a cottage below Cement Shoes Lake and was lending it to us for a couple days.

The sky was cloudy and there was rain in the forecast, but me and my dad didn't mind. On the road, we saw lots of pickups carrying skiffs. During the construction holiday, the mountains were always teeming with people. I remember that as we drove away from town, I started to stress out because I'd be spending three days with my dad and I'd never been alone with him so long. I tried to find topics of conversation in my head. We could talk about school. In the fall, I'd be moved to an advanced class. We could talk about movies. I knew he'd liked *The Last House on the Left*, and I'd watched it the week before. I also knew I didn't want to talk about Kevin.

It was pouring rain when we parked in front of the cottage around dinnertime. The place was a log cabin with a tin roof. My dad's buddy had built it fifty feet from a lake whose name I can't remember. The guy hadn't bought a generator, so we'd use lanterns for light and cook on a little butane stove and on the barbecue. We'd keep our food in our powder-blue Coleman coolers. My dad had brought two—one for the beer, milk, juice and soda, and one for the food. We went inside, and I saw the cottage was just one room with bunk beds along one wall. I asked my dad if I could sleep on the top bunk. He said that since it was my birthday, I could sleep anywhere I wanted. The furniture was just a card table, two chairs covered in flowery yellow plastic, and a wooden bench that looked like a church pew.

That night, it rained nonstop, so we didn't go out on the lake. My dad cooked up some beef-tallow meatballs—his secret recipe. When I was little, he'd always prepare meatballs for me in the woods. He wouldn't reveal what he put in the ground beef to make it taste so good. I knew, though, that he mixed together three different sauces—Diana, Bull's-Eye and HP—and added green peppers and a big Spanish onion. My dad cooked the meatballs on the barbecue despite the rain because otherwise the cottage would reek, he said. I ate two big meatballs and went to bed not long after since I was bushed. In bed, I could hear my dad as he put together and took apart our fishing rods and wondered aloud which spoon lures would work best on Cement

Shoes Lake. I didn't care that the cottage was dinky. In fact, things were going better with my dad than I'd expected.

The only problem was we had to pee and shit in this vile stinky outhouse. All these little black and red beetles crawled around on the shit at the bottom of the hole. I threw tons of lime on the damn things, but it didn't seem to bother them much. They just kept creeping around and eating our poop. It grossed me out so much that I held it in as long as I could before going back to the outhouse after dinner. My dad laughed his head off at me and made up some dumb limerick about a brown-nose beetle named Pierre who loved to climb up your derriere. I'd rarely seen him in such a good mood.

I slept good despite the rain battering our tin roof. When I got up, my dad was making breakfast in his khaki cargo pants and old steel-toe boots. He said it'd poured all night. We sat across from each other to eat our eggs. He'd even gone to the trouble of cooking me some bacon in an aluminum tray despite not wanting any himself. He explained that Cement Shoes was a night lake. You couldn't land a trout before eight in the evening. To get there, we'd cross the little lake next to our cottage and then go up the mountain on the other side. We played cards and dice for a part of the afternoon. I read *Cujo* for an hour or two and then took a nap. We ate hot dogs for dinner. Around seven o'clock, even though it was still raining, we got dressed, took our gear, and then left the cottage. It wasn't raining as hard as in the afternoon, and we had on our yellow raincoats. Anyways, fish would bite more in the rain. We headed down to the little lake and climbed into the skiff. My dad had mounted the motor before dinner, so we sat on our life jackets and set off. While we were crossing the lake, I thought of Eve. Was the weather as shitty in Cape Cod? Was she stuffing herself with lobster? Would she bring me back a souvenir?

When we reached the other side, my dad said we still had a half-hour walk to Cement Shoes Lake. He took the paddles and backpack and had me carry the fishing rods and motor. We started climbing a trail that bordered a stream flowing down the mountain. The trail was really steep, and a zillion goddamn sandflies were buzzing in my ears and trying to bite my head. The outboard weighed like a hundred pounds, I thought I'd die, and our fishing rods kept getting caught in the spruce trees. God, was that trail ever a bitch. I got to the top totally wiped out, and my dad called me a wimp. I was no longer in the mood to fish.

At the boat landing on the lake, my dad started swearing because he couldn't find the key to unlock the chain around the skiff. After ten minutes of cursing, he found the key at the very bottom of his tackle box. We dragged the boat down to the water. I asked if I could turn my flashlight on since there was almost no moon that night. My dad said yeah, but that I should switch it off once we got to our spot on the lake. Using lights to attract fish wasn't allowed.

My dad took out the two life jackets from under the big bench in the skiff. We sat on them and then paddled till the water was deep enough to use the motor. He put the shaft in the water, started the motor up, and then pointed us toward the fishway on the lake.

When we reached our spot, my dad stopped the motor and dropped the anchor overboard. He said there was about fifty feet of water on the boat's left side, but that the lake bottom rose fast on the right. I'd have to cast my line over the side and reel it back fast so it wouldn't get caught on the bottom. I prepared my line and then cast it once. My lure was too heavy to fish in such shallow water, so I asked my dad if I could change it. He nudged the tackle box toward me with his foot. I chose a Toronto Wobbler. With a spoon like that, the fish would be biting for sure.

We must've fished for an hour without exchanging a word. We cast, we reeled. Even though it was raining hard and my hands and knees were all wet, I felt weirdly good. My dad cracked open a beer, took a long gulp, and then set the can down on the bench beside him. While I was reeling in my line, he asked if I liked living in the condo. I didn't know what to say. Maybe it was a trick question. I said yeah, but that we'd be moving to Paul's place at the end of the summer, which kind of sucked. My dad didn't reply right away. He opened his tackle box. He too had changed his lure a half-hour earlier, but still he undid his line and then redid it with a new hook. He chose the fly I'd given him for his fortieth birthday. At the time, I'd been ten years old, and my dad had taught me how to make my own flies. I'd given him an imitation mayfly, and that sucker was perfect for night fishing.

Yet even my mayfly didn't catch anything. It was getting late, probably around ten o'clock, and we'd go back empty-handed. My dad explained that it was because the lake had risen too high. Usually three boulders would stick out of the water over near the outlet, but that night they were totally underwater. In the forty years he'd been fishing in the mountains, he'd never seen a lake so high. He started putting his rod away, so I drew my line in and did the same. I was surprised that he wasn't mad he hadn't caught a single fish.

My dad had something to talk to me about before we headed back. Joanne was moving in with him, he said. They'd decided to close off the basement and turn it into a small two-bedroom apartment with its own separate entrance. His girlfriend found the house too big and had suggested setting up a rental unit downstairs and offering it to me when I was old enough. It'd bring us closer together, she thought. My dad smiled at me and said that at fifteen I was old enough to live alone. With everything I'd gone through in the spring, I'd grown up real fast. Of course, he'd be just upstairs and could keep an eye on me. I had to continue getting good grades, but if I wanted, I could move downstairs in August once the renovations were done. That way, I'd start school already back at his house. He'd give me a weekly allowance to pay for my groceries and everyday expenses, but he'd cover the heating, phone and electricity. I was blown away by his offer, which was like the coolest idea ever. My mom would never go for it, though. My dad said I should let him deal with her, and then he started the motor.

At the boat landing, it was darker than three feet up a black bear's ass. My dad dragged the skiff onto a row of logs. As we were heading off, he asked if I knew why the lake was nicknamed Cement Shoes. I had no clue. There was a biker at the bottom of the lake, my dad said. Joe somebody or other. He'd owed a ton of money to a loan shark in Jonquière and couldn't pay it back, so the shark's henchmen stuck Joe's feet in a washtub filled with cement. They rowed him to the outlet, just where we'd been earlier, and threw him overboard. Nobody ever found the body. The police detectives never came up to the lake to investigate because the loan shark had paid them off good. My dad stopped in his tracks and pointed. He said that if you looked real closely, you'd see Joe's washtub of cement at the bottom of the outlet, provided the water level was low enough and the sun was out. Since it was dark and raining, though, we couldn't see it.

I remember that story really spooked me. We started down the trail, and so much muddy water was running past our feet that it was like it was racing us to the bottom. On the way down, I kept thinking about the dude in the lake. Maybe Joe the biker haunted the nearby woods and the trail, I said to my dad. He laughed and said he wouldn't rule it out. His buddy who owned the cottage had claimed he'd seen some creepy guy wandering the trail. I was afraid of ghosts and spirits, and my dad knew it. He was trying to scare me on purpose. I realized he was kidding around, but for some reason I still freaked. I hightailed it down that trail, practically running the rest of the way. My dad called out to slow down. He didn't want me to slip and hurt myself.

By the time we reached the cottage, I was crying and covered in mud to my knees. I was furious with my dad. He was crazy and horrible, I said. My dad didn't lose his cool. He just told me to pull myself together. I wasn't a child anymore. I had to start acting like a grownup and stop letting my imagination run away with me. To live alone in an apartment, you needed to be an adult. He hoped I wouldn't disappoint him, and he warned that if I wasn't careful, I'd turn into my mom for real. I tried to argue, but he sent me off to bed and said he'd put our stuff out to dry. I was exhausted anyway and itching to get out of my wet clothes. I changed and then climbed to the top bunk. I had trouble falling asleep, though, because the rain was making a racket on our roof.

The next morning, my dad was still in a pretty good mood. He made us eggs, and we ate them watching the rain come down outside. It looked like it'd never stop. Afterward, we packed up our things to go home. There were giant puddles and heavy runoff all around the pickup. The lake near the cottage was insanely high. In the truck, my dad turned on the radio as soon as we drove off. That was when we learned it was the frigging apocalypse in town. The reporter said the Ha! Ha! River and the Mars River had overflowed due to the torrential rains of the past few days. That morning, the two rivers had shifted back into their original paths, creating a torrent of mud that had carried away houses, bridges and roads. Half the town of La Baie was destroyed.

My dad barked a laugh and began talking to the reporter like the guy was right in our pickup. Those fucking idiots from the Alcan plant got what they deserved. You couldn't divert rivers and then expect everything to be fine and dandy. Eventually nature would fight back and bite you in the ass. The Americans were to blame. Everybody in the region knew they were doing experiments on the weather. They manipulated it with low-frequency signals and would use the same technology to win wars. There were magnetic field lines up north, and it was no secret to anybody. They all led directly into Lac St. Jean and Lake Mistassini. To pick up the low-frequency signals, the American army had even bought a farm in Roberval. The mayor had sold it for peanuts, which was no surprise at all since the guy was a crook. That must've been what happened. The Americans had planned a flood, and the entire Saguenay would now pay the price. My dad explained all this while doing 120 down the logging road. Puddles of water were splashing on either side of the pickup, and it was like the Red Sea parting in the catechism book I'd read in second grade.

We drove for a good half-hour more before we reached town. The whole time, the radio was airing reports on the damage. Two meters of water had swept through Chicoutimi, and three people were missing. The Chicoutimi River was out of control, and the Basin district was completely flooded. The army had arrived on the scene. Uprooted houses were floating down rivers that had jumped their banks. The mayor of Chicoutimi and the Canadian army were asking residents to stay home and stock up on drinking water and non-perishables.

While I listened to all this, I was thinking of a hundred things at once. I wondered if Fred could still drive down to Quebec City to get his new batch of PCP. I pictured my mom going to pieces in her condo as she imagined me and my dad drowning in some river. I thought of Eve and prayed her house wouldn't float away.

I glanced at my dad, who'd gone all quiet. He was no doubt worried about his girlfriend. The rain was coming down even harder, and as I looked out the window of the pickup, I couldn't help imagining the water filling up Kevin's coffin and running down his throat. I had to fight back my tears.

My dad said he doubted we could get across the Chicoutimi North bridge, but in the end we managed to reach the other side. Guys from the Bagotville air-force base were there directing traffic and piling sandbags along the exits to the highway. The river by the old paper mill had gone berserk and was dragging along everything in its path. After coming off the bridge, we were stuck for almost an hour in the pickup because the traffic wasn't budging and everybody was rubbernecking. I was afraid that the bridge would collapse and Chicoutimi North would be cut off from the rest of the world. We saw couches, telephone poles, sheds, cars and loads of debris get washed away in the current.

At one point, we heard a thunderous noise, and I thought we were going to die. Just opposite, dozens of houses had been torn from their foundations and came floating toward us down the river. I'd never seen anything like it. The houses drifted closer, and I saw the one that my parents had almost bought when I was a little kid. We'd visited it, but my mom had thought the river was too close and that I might accidentally fall in. I recognized the house right away. It was big with a red roof. My dad was flipping out. He twisted around in his seat so he wouldn't miss a thing. He said we were witnessing a historic moment, and just as he spoke, I saw the house begin to sink, not far from where me and my dad were watching. I climbed out of the pickup just in time to see the house disappear into the Saguenay River.

ESPLANADE
Books

THE FICTION SERIES AT VÉHICULE PRESS

Véhicule Press